Angels in the Outfield

A Novel by Jordan Horowitz
Based on the Motion Picture from Walt Disney Pictures
In association with Caravan Pictures
Executive Producer Gary Stutman
Based on the Motion Picture *Angels in the Outfield* Written for the Screen
  by Dorothy Kingsley & George Wells from the Turner Entertainment Co. Library
Based on the Screenplay by Holly Goldberg Sloan
Produced by Irby Smith Joe Roth and Roger Birnbaum
Directed by William Dear

New York

Library of Congress Catalog Card Number: 94-70250
ISBN: 0-7868-4012-9

Angels in the Outfield

◆ 1 ◆ A View from Above

The two boys sat nestled in the branches of a tree overlooking Anaheim Stadium. From that vantage point they were enjoying the baseball game between the California Angels and the Toronto Blue Jays.

The Angels were in the field, and, as usual, they were losing.

"Geez, they're bad," said ten-year-old Roger Bowman as he watched the game through a pair of binoculars.

"Sooo bad," echoed the other boy. J.P., age six, turned up the volume on the small radio that sat on his lap.

"—and Steve Acker lofts the ball high into left field," came the sportscaster's voice over the radio. "Mitchell and Williams are *both* going for the catch. And it's center fielder Ben Williams's call. And Williams and Mitchell collide and the catch is blown! Spinoza scores! The Blue Jays now lead eight to nothing!

1

Nineteen-year-old Williams once again lacks the confidence to take command in the outfield. And Williams is finally able to get the ball to Garcia at short, holding Acker at third. And with this latest disaster, manager George Knox heads to the mound to have a word with his pitcher, Frank Gates."

"I don't think it's gonna be a happy word," sighed Roger, watching the slightly paunchy Angels manager emerge from the dugout and march toward the pitcher's mound.

"Uh-uh, not a happy word," agreed J.P. Then his face brightened with hope. "But they could still win! It *could* happen!"

Roger looked doubtful as he continued to focus his binoculars on the goings-on below. The Angels manager was now standing in front of the pitcher, flailing his arms angrily. He motioned for the pitcher to hand over the ball and return to the dugout. Instead, the pitcher defiantly threw the ball into the stands. A second later, he threw his glove there, too.

Suddenly the manager lunged at the pitcher's throat.

"They're fighting now," said Roger.

"I hate fighting," said J.P.

Roger grimaced. "But it's the one thing they're good at," he quipped.

When Roger focused his binoculars again,

he saw that the rest of the Angels players were now rushing in from the outfield. Still more were coming off the bench. Within seconds the entire team had reached the pitcher's mound to join in the fight.

"This is *outrageous!*" the sportscaster shouted frantically. "The whole Angels team is now in a brawl, with skipper George Knox in the center! I don't think I've ever seen a manager fight off his *own* players! And here comes the umpire. Here come *two* umpires. Here come *all the* umpires! And as the skirmish is broken up, manager Knox is *thrown out* of the ballpark! He'll watch the rest of the game from the locker room!"

"Again," sighed Roger.

"Again," J.P. repeated sadly.

Things shortly settled down on the field. Through his binoculars Roger saw the Angels return to their positions. A new pitcher took the mound.

"Come on," Roger muttered as if he were whispering into the pitcher's ear. "Strike him out." The Angels were his home team and he wanted to see them win.

"Yeah, strike him out," echoed J.P. Then that big, hopeful smile spread across his face again. "It *could* happen!"

"HEY, WHAT'RE YOU KIDS DOING UP THERE?!" came an angry voice from below.

Roger and J.P. snapped their eyes downward. A security guard, from the top row of the stadium stands, had spotted the boys watching the game for free.

"Game's over for us!" said Roger. "Get goin', J.P.!"

The two boys scurried down the trunk of the tree and dropped onto the soft dirt outside the stadium wall. Then they scrambled over a hill and across a parking lot. At the edge of the parking lot, a fence with a faded metal sign read Authorized Angels Personnel Only. The edge of the sign was bent all out of shape. Roger and J.P. lifted the bent sign and squeezed through the fence. A shallow moat of water now separated them from a yard that led to the main street. A wide pipe was suspended over the water. The boys hopped onto the pipe and started across it.

SPLASH! Suddenly something landed in the muddy water beside them. Roger looked down and saw a baseball bobbing up and down. Roger figured the ball must be courtesy of the Blue Jays. The Angels were being slaughtered for certain.

Roger bent down, plucked the ball out of the water, and wiped it dry on his pants. He

4

wanted to keep it as a souvenir. But when he saw that J.P. was looking at him, eyes wide with envy, he tossed the ball to his little friend.

"Can I really have it?" asked J.P. with disbelief.

"It's yours," smiled Roger. "C'mon. We gotta hurry and get back before Maggie gets mad."

In a few minutes the boys reached a pile of underbrush and pulled out two old bicycles that they had hidden there before sneaking into Anaheim Stadium. The boys hopped on the bikes and pedaled away.

2 ◆ School of Hard Knox

The Angels lost to the Blue Jays, 10–0.

After the game, the players quickly left the field. As the Angels filed into the locker room, one by one they reached out and touched a spot on the pillar that stood just inside the door. The paint on the pillar was worn away from being rubbed so many times in the same place. When Jose Martinez, the second baseman, walked in, he removed a wad of gum from his mouth, stuck it on the pillar, and then gave it a ceremonial swat.

"Why do you idiots do that after we've lost?" asked Frank Gates, the pitcher who had been pulled out of the game after the big brawl on the field.

"It's for good luck," said Ray Mitchell, the left fielder who had collided with Williams earlier.

"Maybe we should do it *before* we lose," quipped pitcher Whit Bass. He had just hit

6

the pillar and was now staring at his gum-covered hand.

Danny Hemmerling, the utility infielder from New York and resident expert on the history of baseball, entered the locker room and swatted the pillar. "After fifteen straight losses I say we find something else to touch," he sighed.

Just then Triscuit "the Mountain" Messmer squeezed between Hemmerling and the pillar. Messmer was huge. He stood a head above the other players and was twice as wide. He also sported a Mohawk.

"Comin' through!" shouted Messmer as he charged into the center of the room. He headed straight for the table piled high with postgame drinks and sandwiches.

"Aw, not again!" he groaned. "They got the wrong kinda salami!"

Mitchell and Hemmerling opened a door marked Treatment Room. It was the room where the players could treat the various aches and pulled muscles they got during the game.

Mel Clark, at thirty-eight the oldest pitcher on the club, sat in a whirlpool bathtub in the middle of the room. His deeply lined face showed his years. His pitching arm was in a support sling that he kept submerged in the warm, soothing water. A lit cigarette dangled from his lips.

"How's the arm?" Hemmerling asked Clark.

Clark smiled unconvincingly. "Feeling stronger," he answered.

"Mel," said Mitchell, "you'll be pitching no-hitters any day now."

Clark nodded at Mitchell. He then let out a harsh cough, the result of too many years of smoking cigarettes.

"ONE MORE LOSS!!!" a voice bellowed from behind. Hemmerling and Mitchell spun around. George Knox had just entered the locker room and he was mad—steaming mad.

"One more loss that could have been a WIN!!!" Knox continued to scream. The players cowered. Knox's eyes were full of rage and his muscles tense with anger. He stormed over to the food table, reached down, and flipped it upside down in one fell swoop.

"You call yourselves professionals?!" Knox said to the players accusingly. "I have never, EVER seen a worse group of players! You don't think as a team! You don't play as a team! One more loss and I'll—I'll—I'll do *this to you!*"

And with that, Knox picked up a chair and hurled it across the room. The chair crashed into a bat cart. The players ran for cover as the bats torpedoed in all directions.

"I want you here, in uniform, at nine o'clock tomorrow," demanded Knox. "We're going back to work on fundamentals!"

Danny Hemmerling slowly rose from behind a bench. "Fundamentals in the middle of the season?" he asked timidly.

"I thought the game started at one," Whit Bass added meekly.

"It *does* start at one!" Knox barked at the pitcher. "You lamebrain!"

And with that, Knox stormed out of the locker room and down the tunnel that led back to the field. He was so angry that he almost didn't see the tall elderly man walking down the tunnel toward him. The man, in his seventies, wore a Western suit and cowboy hat.

"Tough loss, George," said Hank Murphy, an ex–movie star who now owned the team.

"I can't take it anymore!" Knox moaned to Murphy. "You gotta start trading them! All of them! Now!"

"I can't trade twenty-five players," explained Murphy.

"Sure you can," replied Knox. "Besides, these guys aren't players."

"A lot of 'em are just young. Green. It takes time."

"And the rest of them are old. Gray. Hopefully they'll die. Soon. Like tonight!"

"George, now really . . ."

Knox looked pleadingly at his boss. "I can't *win* with these guys," he said. "No one could. There's such a thing called *talent*. They don't have any!"

"This isn't Cincinnati, George," said Murphy. He was referring to the Cincinnati Reds, the team Knox had managed before the Angels. "No one expects you to win big with these boys. Now, I thought the reason you took this job was to ease up a little. Especially after last year."

"I came here to manage a winning ball team," Knox snapped back. He didn't want to be reminded of last year, the year he was fired from the Reds.

Murphy studied Knox's face. At one time Knox had been one of baseball's best managers. But over the last few years his temper had grown worse, and so had his judgment.

"All right," agreed Murphy. "If it'll make you feel better, I'll trade a player. Just tell me which one."

"It's so hard to choose," Knox said as the names of the players went through his mind.

"Hang on, partner," Murphy said, patting

10

Knox on the back. "You'll ride through the dark days."

Murphy walked off, leaving Knox to ponder the decision of who would be traded from the team. Frustrated, Knox slammed his foot into a nearby trash can, sending the can and its contents streaming across the tunnel. The can nearly rolled into a young man in a crisp suit. The young man was holding a clipboard and a bullhorn.

"Mr. Knox," said the young man. "You're scheduled to do Ranch Wilder's postgame show. He's waiting."

"The press are all scum," Knox told the young man. "They're meant to be kept waiting. And Ranch Wilder is worse than scum. Who are you, anyway?"

"Your new assistant, David Montaine." David extended his hand to Knox. Knox ignored it and started out of the tunnel toward the field.

"What happened to Barney, or Baily, or whatever the jerk's name was?" asked Knox.

David followed behind Knox. "You fired him," he reminded his new boss. "They hired me Monday."

Knox threw David an unfriendly look. "Then I can't fire you until Friday," he told him. "Make a note."

David nervously adjusted his tie and began

writing on his clipboard. "It's been noted," he said, realizing that all the awful things he had heard about George Knox were true.

Knox walked out of the tunnel and into the stadium. A cluster of technicians was huddled around home plate setting up video cameras and lights. In the center stood Ranch Wilder, the sportscaster who announced all the Angels games. Wilder's assistant, Wally, hurried over to Knox and quickly clipped a microphone to his uniform.

"Thrown out of the game," Wilder said privately to Knox. "I imagine the commissioner's fine will be hefty."

Knox threw Wilder a hard look. The two men had known each other for many years. Wilder had seen Knox in his best days as a player and a coach. Now he was seeing him at his worst.

"We're on in three seconds," said Wally.

Wilder looked straight into one of the video cameras. Suddenly his manner became sharp and professional. "And we're back with Angels manager George Knox," Wilder said, looking straight into the camera lens. "This was a hard loss today."

"Any loss is hard," replied Knox with a slight grumble in his voice.

"But this one really got to you," insisted

Wilder. "You leave Cincinnati after ten years of winning ball clubs—although the really big one seemed just out of reach—and you come out to manage our Angels. Expectations were high that you could turn things around, but it seems that's just not going to happen."

"Season's only half over, Ranch," defended Knox.

"And your club's in last place."

"You ought to know how one incident can change the course of events," replied Knox. Knox was reminding Wilder of an incident when they were both pro ball players years before. Wilder had spiked Knox's knee during a slide. The injury caused Knox to give up playing baseball forever.

"You play the game, you take your chances," Wilder snapped back. "Sometimes you're in the wrong place at the wrong time."

"You're an expert on that!" shouted Knox.

"I could say the same about you!" yelled Wilder.

"You've said worse!" Knox yelled louder.

By now the producer was signaling for the two men to stop arguing. She pulled at some wires and handed a microphone to Wally, motioning for him to take over.

"Are we off the air?" asked Wilder once he saw that Wally was continuing the broadcast.

"Great," said Knox. "And since I'm already going to be fined by the commissioner. . . ."

Knox clenched his fist and threw a punch squarely into Wilder's face. Wilder went down, and the impact kicked up clouds of dirt around home plate. Knox rubbed his fist, then turned and walked out of the stadium. When he was sure no one was looking, he broke into a victorious smile.

◆ 3 ◆ Maggie's House

It was starting to get dark by the time Roger and J.P. pedaled up to the foster home where they lived. Like many of the other houses in the neighborhood, this one had protective bars on the windows and graffiti on the fences.

Maggie Nelson, the boys' caretaker, was standing on the porch waiting for them. By the look on her face the boys knew that they were late.

"Where've you been?" Maggie demanded as she started down the walkway toward the garage.

J.P. looked down at the pavement. He was trying to hide his guilty expression.

"Just ridin' around the block, Maggie," explained Roger, but Maggie knew he wasn't telling the whole truth.

"You said you'd be back by five o'clock," she said.

"I can't tell time yet," added J.P. "Is it five o'clock?"

"Close," said Maggie in that forgiving tone of hers. "Put the bikes away."

Maggie watched as Roger and J.P. locked their bikes up in the garage.

"I'm starving," said Roger as he closed the garage door. "What are we havin' for dinner?"

"Macaroni and cheese," answered Maggie.

"My mom used to make macaroni and cheese," said Roger.

"Mine, too, I think," said J.P. "I don't really know." J.P. was too young to remember.

"I'm sure she did," Roger told his friend. "All moms do."

With their stomachs growling, the two boys made a start for the house. But Maggie put her arm on J.P.'s shoulders, gently holding him back.

"Honey, you stay with me," she told the younger boy. "Roger's got a visitor inside."

Suddenly Roger's face lit up. He broke away from Maggie and J.P., ran up the porch steps, and burst into the little house. In the shadows of the living room stood a man in his early thirties.

It was Roger's dad.

"Surprised to see me?" his dad asked.

Roger nodded.

"You look kinda scrawny," said his dad. "They feed you enough in this place?"

"Yeah."

"Where you been? I was waitin'."

"Watching the baseball game."

"Angels still your team?"

"Yeah."

"They still in last place?"

"Yeah."

Roger's dad grinned. It was a bitter grin. "Runs in the blood," he said. "A family that likes losers."

Roger and his father looked at each other in silence. Although young, his dad had a tired and beaten look about him. Roger didn't know why, but he suddenly felt very sad.

"I've come to say I'm goin' up north," his dad told him, breaking the silence. "I know I said when I came it'd be to get you, but things ain't workin' out that way. I done what I could with you. Maybe if your mom was alive it'd be different. They had me sign a paper. A release kinda thing. It's got to go to the court to be final. You understand what I'm saying, don't you?"

Roger was looking down at the floor. His foot was edging into a worn spot on the carpet, making the hole bigger. "Yeah," he answered, although he really didn't understand at all.

"Okay then," his father said with a sigh of relief. "We got that out of the way."

After another few seconds of silence Roger

17

followed his father out of the house and watched him mount a battered motorcycle that was parked at the curb.

"What happened to the pickup?" Roger asked. In the years before his mother passed away, their old pickup truck had been the family car. Now his dad had a motorcycle.

"Traded it in," answered his father. "The bike's better for travelin'."

"Dad," Roger began hesitantly. "When do you think I'll have a family?"

Roger's dad looked off into the horizon. He knew he couldn't make the boy any promises. So far he had broken every one he'd ever made. He noticed the baseball stadium in the distance and grinned.

"From where I sit," he began thoughtfully, "I'd say when the Angels win the pennant." Then he revved the bike and released the throttle. "Stay outta trouble, kid." And with that, he pulled away from the curb and drove down the street.

Roger continued to stare down the street after his father had disappeared from sight. He hoped that if he stood there long enough, his father might change his mind and come back. But after awhile, Roger went back into the house.

* * *

Roger joined Maggie and J.P. at the kitchen table for dinner. Even though the macaroni and cheese smelled delicious, Roger was too upset to eat. All he could think about was his father.

A third boy, Miguel, sat at the table with them. A couple of years older than Roger, Miguel was tough, really tough.

"Tomorrow your social worker is picking you up for an interview," Maggie said to Miguel. "She'll be here by eleven o'clock."

"Good," Miguel said flatly. "I didn't want to go to the baseball game anyway. The Angels never win."

"I want to go to the game," said J.P. excitedly. "They *could* win."

"And you could get a stomachache after dinner from food poisoning," Miguel shot back at J.P.

"Leave him alone," Roger warned Miguel. Miguel may have been tough, but Roger wasn't going to let anybody pick on his little friend.

"Boys, stop it," said Maggie. Then she got up from the table. "We have Jell-O for dessert."

J.P.'s face exploded with a big-time smile. "Jell-O! YAAAYYY!"

Miguel leaned over. "It's not really Jell-O," he whispered to J.P. "It's cat brains with food coloring. She kills 'em at night and feeds 'em to us to save money."

J.P. looked scared.

"Shut up!" Roger snapped at Miguel. He was ready for a fight.

"Roger, we don't use language like that in this house!" yelled Maggie as she pulled a bowl of wiggling pink Jell-O from the refrigerator.

"Sorry," said Roger.

Maggie returned to the table and served the Jell-O. Miguel watched as J.P. dug a spoon deep into his bowl. Then he meowed like a cat as the little boy put the heaping spoonful into his mouth.

Several hours later the three boys climbed into their beds. As was her nightly custom, Maggie watched from the doorway of the bedroom.

"You washed your faces," she began as usual. "Brushed your teeth. You went to the bathroom. You picked out the lint between your toes. You said your prayers."

"Yeah," said all three boys at once.

"Good night, boys," said Maggie. Then she turned off the bedroom light and quietly shut the door.

"I didn't brush my teeth," said Miguel as soon as Maggie was gone.

"What's lint again?" asked J.P.

"I didn't wash my face," added Roger.

The three boys giggled mischievously.

"Why have we got to sleep in sleeping bags?" asked J.P. He always had trouble zipping his bag closed at night.

"She makes us sleep in sleeping bags because she's too old to bend over and tuck in the sheets," said Miguel.

"She is not too old," insisted Roger. "She's just got lots to do."

"Did you guys pray?" J.P. asked.

"I pray every night you'll go to sleep instead of bugging us with a thousand stupid questions," Miguel snapped back.

"Maybe tomorrow you'll meet a nice family, Miguel," said J.P. "I'll pray for that. It *could* happen!"

"Go to sleep, nuthead," said Miguel in his best tough voice. "And don't worry about me. Worry about yourself."

J.P. and Miguel closed their eyes and drifted into sleep, but Roger was too restless to sleep. Instead, he stared out the window next to his bed and thought about his father.

He wondered why his father had left him. Had he done something wrong—something that made his father not want him? He had always tried to be a good boy. Maybe he just wasn't good enough, he thought. He wished there was something he could do to make his father take him back.

He wanted so much to have a family again.

Through the window he could see the moon and the stars and the sky. Below them he could see Anaheim Stadium.

What was it his father had said to him just before riding away? That Roger would have a family again if the Angels won the pennant? Roger pouted as he remembered the way the Angels had played earlier that day. Those guys couldn't win a game, let alone the playoffs, he thought to himself.

That would take a miracle.

Roger looked up from the baseball stadium and back into the starlit sky. His eyes began to glisten.

"If there's a God," he prayed quietly, "if you're a man, or a woman . . . if you're listening . . . I'd like to have a family. My dad said that'd happen when the Angels won the pennant. The Angels baseball team, I mean. So, could you work on them? Maybe help them win a little bit?

"Amen . . . A woman, too," Roger finished. Then he dropped his head back onto his pillow and fell asleep. Outside, the stars in the sky began twinkling.

◆ 4 ◆ Sparkling Pajamas

George Knox stood outside Hank Murphy's office and looked at the door. He knew why the boss wanted to see him, but he didn't want to force it. Lately it seemed as if he couldn't make a single move without upsetting somebody.

After a few minutes Knox gently knocked on the door and entered the office.

"You want to see me?" he asked.

Hank Murphy was sitting behind his desk aiming a remote control at a television set across the room. He was watching a replay of yesterday's game—the one in which Knox got into a brawl with the entire team.

"Feelin' any better today, George?" Murphy asked his manager.

"Why would I feel better?" asked Knox.

"The commissioner fined you five thousand dollars for jumping Gates," Murphy reminded Knox. "And Ranch Wilder is gonna press civil charges for popping him."

"Come to think of it, I have felt better since I slugged Wilder," Knox said with a grin. "I hadn't made the connection."

Murphy threw Knox a serious stare. "Your pistol's smokin', pal," he commented.

"I'll cover the fine. And Wilder."

"That's not the point," said Murphy as he clicked off the television set. "Look, I know you and Wilder have been at each other's throats since you were players."

"We've been at each other's throats since he spiked my knee and wrecked my career," Knox corrected his boss.

"Accidents happen, George."

"It wasn't an accident. When you slide into a catcher with your nails up it's on purpose."

"That was fifteen years ago," said Murphy. "You're both still in the same business. And now you're with the same team. You should support each other!"

"I'd rather eat dirt," insisted Knox. "I was just coming into my best years. If I hadn't been injured by that slime, we'd have won the pennant!"

"And if you hadn't lost control of your team last season, Cincinnati would have won the pennant. Isn't that so?"

A hard expression came over Knox's face as he remembered last season.

"I don't want to talk about the past," he said flatly.

Murphy was growing impatient. "Don't go making more mud pies to step in," he told Knox. "Control yourself today."

Knox agreed to keep his temper under control and left Murphy's office. As soon as he was outside he knew that he wouldn't be able to keep his promise. It wasn't just Ranch Wilder or last season's playoff failure that he was angry about. It wasn't even the ragtag Angels ball club that got him steamed. He was just angry at everyone and everything.

George Knox was an unhappy man.

Batting practice had begun by the time Knox returned to the field. Mel Clark, his arm no longer in the sling, approached Knox.

"Trainer says I'm ready to pitch," Clark told Knox. "When do I get off the bench?"

"How does never sound," replied Knox bluntly. "You're here 'cuz you got a contract that pays you to be here. You blew out your arm. Played on too many pain pills."

"Too many pain pills?" repeated Clark with astonishment. "You're the one who shoved them down my throat five years ago in Cincinnati!"

"Hey," Knox snapped back. "It was your

25

decision to swallow 'em. I had a brain. When you were finished I traded you. I never thought I'd get stuck with you again."

Clark was furious. But when he opened his mouth to reply he began to cough. His coughing fit was so violent his face turned bright red.

"Out of my way," said Knox. "I got a ball club to manage."

Knox pushed past Clark, stormed over to the dugout, and sat down on the bench. He didn't say a single word to anyone for the rest of the practice.

Later a bright yellow bus pulled up to the curb in front of Anaheim Stadium. A stream of kids, all of them from foster homes, were led off the bus by several adult social workers.

Among them were Roger and J.P. Today they were part of the local Social Services' field trip. For a change, they didn't have to sneak into the park or climb a tree to see the game.

As soon as the adults settled the excited kids into a row of bleacher seats, Roger grabbed J.P. by the T-shirt.

"C'mon," he said, and led J.P. to a couple of empty seats closer to the field.

Suddenly a hush fell over the stadium. Everyone rose to their feet as the national anthem was played over the loudspeakers. When it was over everyone sat back down.

"GET OUT YOUR TICKET STUBS, EVERYONE," came an announcement. "BECAUSE WE'LL BE GIVING OUT SOUVENIRS THROUGHOUT THE GAME. OUR FIRST PRIZE TODAY IS AN AUTOGRAPHED TEAM BAT TO SECTION 219, ROW J, SEAT 8."

"Wow!" shouted J.P. as he looked at his ticket stub. "I almost won!"

Roger read the numbers on J.P.'s stub and said, "Only the last number matches."

"Yeah," said J.P. with that optimistic big-time smile of his. "But that's *real* close!"

Roger grinned. Nothing ever seemed to disappoint J.P.

Soon the Angels streamed out onto the field to begin their game against the Toronto Blue Jays. The team was met by lukewarm applause from the stands.

The first few innings were uneventful. Neither team scored. Roger, watching from the stands, was quickly growing tired. The game was boring. The Angels weren't losing, but they weren't winning, either.

By the top of the fifth inning the score was still 0–0. Whit Bass was on the pitcher's mound. He wound up and fired the first pitch, straight and fast, toward home plate. The Blue

Jays batter connected, and the ball went sailing high into the air toward the outfield.

It was a deep hit. Roger's eyes narrowed and followed the ball. Ben Williams was playing shallow. He ran after the ball as fast as he could, but it looked like an impossible catch.

Just then Roger noticed two small, fluffy clouds in the sky over the stadium. They had not moved since the game began. Suddenly the two clouds swooped down toward the outfield. By the time they reached Williams they had transformed themselves into two shimmering figures. The figures lifted Williams, one by each arm, and carried him toward the oncoming baseball. With one arm extended, Williams made the catch in midair. Then the figures lowered him back onto the field and returned to the sky.

The crowd cheered wildly at the unexpected catch.

"Holy cow!!!!" exclaimed Roger at the fantastic sight. He searched the field frantically with his eyes, but the shimmering figures had vanished just as quickly as they had appeared.

"Yeah!" echoed J.P. "Holy cow!"

"Did you see that?" Roger asked J.P.

"Yeah!" replied J.P. excitedly. "Awesome!"

"They came right down from the sky!"

J.P. looked at Roger quizzically. "Who?" he asked.

"The guys carrying him," said Roger, pointing at the field and flapping his arms as if they were wings. "The ones in the sparkling pajamas!"

"What are you talking about, Roger?" J.P. asked quietly.

"You didn't see 'em?" asked Roger. "The things pulling Williams?"

J.P. looked back toward the field. "I dunno...," he replied hesitantly.

Roger turned and grabbed the arm of the man sitting next to him. He was a big man with lots of hair on his arms and hands.

"Mister!" said Roger. "Mister, did you see that?!"

"What a play!" said the hairy man.

"But did you see what just happened with the clouds?" insisted Roger. "Did you see the things with Williams when he caught the ball?"

"Huh?" said the hairy man. He had no idea what Roger was talking about.

"There were shiny people out there!" said Roger. "Flying shiny people!"

The man smirked at Roger. "Tell your parents about it," he said, and turned back to the game.

"You guys didn't see them?"

"It was a good play, Roger," said J.P. "I saw that."

Roger sank back into his seat. No one believed him. Not even J.P. He wondered if he could have dreamed the whole thing.

"Amazing play," said the man sitting in the seat beside him. "I love it when they come from above like that."

Roger turned and looked up, expecting to see the same hairy man he had just spoken to. Only now the hairy man was gone and a man with a head full of wild hair was sitting in his seat.

"From above?" asked Roger. He wanted to make sure that he had heard this fellow correctly.

"The sky deal," said the man in a friendly tone. "It's a good entrance for them."

"For whom?" asked Roger cautiously.

"The angels," replied the man.

"You saw 'em?"

" 'Course I saw them," answered the man. "They're with me. The little one's a rookie. He just got off his training wings."

"Those were *real* angels?"

"Accept no substitutes," said the man. "The name's Al. No one can see me or hear me but you."

"Why me?"

"You asked for help, remember? And we're here! We'll come and go. It's an as-needed situation."

"What are you talking about?" asked Roger.

Al glanced down the row of seats. The hairy man was returning to his seat, holding a tray of food.

"Uh-oh, tubby's back," he said. "I'm vapor." Suddenly Al began to disappear into thin air.

"Keep your nose clean and your heart open," Al said to Roger as his voice grew faint. "You got angels around, sonny. We'll be in touch!"

And with that, Al vanished completely just as the hairy man sat back down in his seat. Roger looked at the hairy man, his eyes still wide with bewilderment.

"What's your problem?" asked the hairy man as he started to take a bite out of a hot dog. "You sick or somethin'?"

"Yeah," said Roger in a stunned voice. "Maybe."

Roger turned back to the game, but his thoughts were lost in a whirl of confusion. What did Al mean when he said Roger had asked for help? Then Roger suddenly remembered his prayer from the night before. All at

31

once he realized that Al may have come down to help the Angels win the pennant.

And if the Angels won the pennant, that meant . . .

Now Roger smiled to himself. He knew why the angels had come.

5 ◆ Believing in Angels

By the bottom of the ninth inning the score was still 0–0. Roger knew it was the Angels' last chance to put away the Jays before the game went into extra innings. All they needed was one home run. But when he saw Triscuit Messmer get up to bat he began to worry. Messmer was one of the worst hitters on the team. If anybody needed help from Al's angels, it was him.

Roger had seen no sign of Al's angels since they had helped Ben Williams make that catch in the outfield four innings earlier. Now Roger was beginning to doubt whether he had really seen them at all.

He watched closely as Triscuit Messmer stood at home plate, his bat poised. The batter shuffled nervously to and fro, creating a dirt cloud around his feet. After a few seconds Roger thought he saw something form inside the dust cloud. Leaning forward for a better look, he soon became certain.

An angel was beginning to take form.

"They're back," Roger muttered half out loud.

Then the pitch came. Messmer pulled his bat back and stepped in for the swing. Roger watched with amazement at what happened next. The angel reached his arms around and held on to the bat with Messmer.

Messmer swung stronger and more even than ever before. CRACK! His swing was so powerful that his bat broke in two as it hit the ball. The ball went soaring across the field, over the heads of the visiting team and into the stands.

It was a home run!

The Angels had won their first game since the All-Star break!

The crowd jumped out of their seats and roared with excitement as Messmer huffed and puffed his way around the bases.

Roger turned to J.P. "You didn't see the guy with him?" he asked excitedly. "The angel who swung with Triscuit?"

"We won!!!" exclaimed J.P., who was jumping up and down.

"There are angels in the outfield!" shouted Roger. "And the infield! *Real* ones!"

"OUR FINAL DRAWING," came the stadium announcer's voice over the loudspeaker,

"WILL GIVE THREE LUCKY WINNERS A CHANCE TO BE PHOTOGRAPHED WITH ANGELS MANAGER GEORGE KNOX! THE FIRST WINNER IS IN SECTION 139, AISLE H, SEAT 8!"

J.P. was looking down at his ticket stub as the numbers were called. "I won," he said with surprise. He showed the stub to Roger. This time the numbers *did* match. J.P. had won.

"You do it," J.P. told Roger. "I don't want to have my picture taken. I don't like strangers."

Roger and J.P. found a stadium usher and showed him the ticket. The usher led the two boys down from the stands and onto the baseball field. Some other kids with winning ticket-stub numbers were gathered around watching as the Angels players filed past them toward the locker room.

"Who's he?" asked J.P. He was pointing to Mel Clark.

"I'm not sure," said Roger.

"You kids don't know your baseball," said the usher. "That's Mel Clark."

Suddenly Roger remembered the name. "Mel Clark pitched three shutouts in a row in 1978 for Cincinnati. He was a great player!"

Clark looked over when he heard Roger's excited voice.

35

"Wow," said J.P. "You used to be Mel Clark."

Clark smiled. "Yeah," he said in a sad voice. "I used to be." Then he turned and continued on his way.

"First kid!" called David Montaine. J.P. slid behind Roger and pushed him forward in his place. Then David grabbed Roger by the collar and placed him right next to Knox.

Knox was just standing there motionless. He was looking away, his lips tightened in an angry expression as if he didn't want to be there at all.

In a funny way Roger felt the same. After all, it was J.P. who had won the contest, not him. Now both he and Knox refused to smile for the photographer.

"This looks like a prison photo," said the photographer, peeking out from behind his camera. "Would either of you consider smiling? The team did just win."

"It was a mistake," growled Knox. "This team can't win."

Roger looked up at Knox. "They won because there were angels out there," he said. "Real ones. I saw them. Two angels came out of the sky and picked up Williams. And another angel helped Triscuit Messmer hit a home run. That's why the bat broke."

Knox rolled his eyes in a pained expression. "A psycho kid," he moaned. "Great. David! You'd think they'd screen these people!"

"It's true!" insisted Roger. "Ask Williams about it. Or Messmer. They'll tell you somethin' was goin' on! You'll see!"

Just then the photographer took the picture. Before he could say any more Roger was pulled away from Knox's side and replaced with another kid.

Roger sighed, remembering the look on Knox's face when he told him about the angels. He knew it sounded crazy, but he also knew that it was the truth.

He wondered if anyone would ever believe him.

That evening George Knox sat in his living room filled with sports pictures, equipment, and promotional products, all from his past. He was eating a frozen dinner and watching the recap of the day's game that he had taped from the sports segment on the evening news.

Of course, the big news of the day were the two amazing plays that had given the Angels their victory. Knox watched as the broadcast showed Ben Williams, at the top of the fifth inning, running after the ball, leaping into the air, and making the catch.

It was so good the broadcaster ran it again.

Knox hit the pause button on his remote control and stared at the image on the television set. Ben Williams was *completely* airborne. He was defying the laws of gravity. And his elbows were angled high behind his shoulders. It was almost as if someone had grabbed hold of his arms and was lifting him toward the ball.

"Something's not right," Knox muttered to himself.

Something's not right, George Knox repeated in his mind. Not right at all.

That night Roger lay in bed with his eyes wide open. He couldn't sleep. He was thinking of the events of the day and wondering if it had all been a dream. Had angels really come? Was it even possible?

Everyone thought he was crazy. Even J.P., who was usually full of hope about so many impossible things, seemed to have doubts.

Roger thought Maggie would know if he was crazy or not. He climbed out of bed and went into the living room, where he knew Maggie would be hunched over her sewing machine mending a neighbor's clothes for extra money.

"Why aren't you asleep, honey?" asked Maggie as she looked up from her work.

"Do you believe in angels?" Roger asked her.

"What do angels have to do with your being out of bed?" asked Maggie.

"I want to know," continued Roger. "Do you think they're real?"

Maggie paused for a moment.

"I think there are many, many amazing things in life that we can't explain," she began thoughtfully. "So, yes. I guess I believe in angels. And in miracles. I think the possibility of wondrous things is what makes every day of your life worth waking up for."

Roger smiled. "Me, too," he said happily. "Good night, Maggie."

Roger turned and walked back down the hall to his room. He still couldn't fall asleep so he walked over to the window and stared out at the starry sky. He was smiling. He realized that he hadn't dreamed the amazing events at the baseball game. He wasn't crazy.

Maybe he would have a family after all.

6 ◆ An Invitation to the Game

"They just told me I've been traded to New York!" Frank Gates burst into the stadium video room, where George Knox was watching a replay of yesterday's game.

"Yup," said Knox without even looking up. "If you can make it there, you can make it anywhere."

Gates was furious. He knew the team was in bad shape, but he also knew that it wasn't his fault. What the Angels needed was a better manager, not better players.

"I got two questions!" began Gates. "How many players did you get for me? And did you make the ball club any better?"

"Zero players," answered Knox. "And yes, the club's better."

Gates snarled. "We all hate you," he told Knox. "You know that, right?"

"It's mutual," Knox replied flatly.

"You may have had winning teams when

you managed Cincinnati," said Gates, "but you'll never have a winning club here! It would take an act of God for that to happen!"

Gates stormed out of the room, slamming the door behind him.

Knox was too busy looking at the video monitor to be concerned about Gates. He watched Ben Williams fly into the air again to make yesterday's catch. Then Knox fast-forwarded the tape and studied the way Triscuit Messmer slammed the ball that broke his bat in two.

He stared at the image for a long moment. An act of God, he thought to himself, remembering Gates's last words to him.

And with that, he picked up the telephone and called Ben Williams.

An hour later there was a knock on Knox's office door. Ben Williams, still in his street clothes, walked in.

"Nice catch yesterday, Ben," said Knox, who was sitting behind his desk.

"Thanks," said Williams.

"How'd it feel?" asked Knox. "Or was it so fast you don't even remember?"

Williams thought about yesterday's game. He hadn't mentioned it to anybody yet, but he had a funny feeling about that catch. "I felt weightless," he told Knox. "Almost like someone had me by the arms. Like I was being lifted. I never felt that before."

A few minutes later Knox walked downstairs to the locker room. Triscuit Messmer was at his usual pregame spot, stuffing his mouth with food from the snack table. Knox asked Messmer the same question he had asked Williams. Then he waited for Messmer to swallow.

"It wasn't a regular homer," Messmer finally explained. "Nope. It felt like someone was swinging with me. Very strange. I could feel some added power comin' from somewhere. Maybe it was the chili dog I had before the game."

That was all that Knox needed to hear. He reached for the locker room telephone and called David Montaine. Within minutes his assistant gave him the information he needed: Roger Bowman's name and home address.

Knox pulled up in front of Maggie's house and got out. In his hands was a manila envelope containing the photograph that was taken of him and Roger at yesterday's game. He walked up to the front door and rang the doorbell. A moment later Maggie appeared.

"Yes?" she asked Knox.

"I'm looking for Roger Bowman," said Knox. "Does he live here?"

"Yes," replied Maggie.

"I'm George Knox from the Angels. Roger won a photograph at Friday's game."

Maggie reached for the envelope, but Knox held it tight.

"Is he around?" asked Knox.

"Did he do something wrong?" Maggie asked suspiciously.

"No," replied Knox. "I'd just like to talk with him."

"He's out on his bike," explained Maggie.

"When will he be back?"

"I'm not sure," answered Maggie. "But I can give him the picture."

"No," said Knox anxiously. "I'd like to give it to him myself."

Maggie let Knox into the house. He sat in a chair and waited as Maggie went back to her work at the sewing machine.

"You're Roger's mom?" asked Knox.

"No."

"Aunt? Grandma?"

"I'm no relation," explained Maggie. "This is a short-term foster care facility. I run it. Roger is a ward of the state."

"Oh," said Knox. "So, Roger—he's got a wild imagination? Always making up stories?"

"No," answered Maggie. "He's very grounded in reality. Most children who are

43

taken away from their parents by the court system have a good handle on reality."

"I bet."

Maggie took her foot off the sewing machine pedal and looked at Knox. She suspected he wanted more than to give Roger some photograph. "What do you want from him?" she asked. "Why are you really here?"

"Young fans," answered Knox, fearful that Maggie would throw him out if he told her the truth. "We need more of them."

Just then Knox and Maggie heard the sound of two bicycles pedaling up the front walk. Knox went to the front door and stepped outside. Roger and J.P. were parking their bikes. When they finished they saw Knox standing on the front porch.

Both boys were surprised.

"Hey," said Knox awkwardly. He held out the envelope. "I got your picture."

Roger took the envelope. "Thanks," he said. "I didn't know you were going to bring it."

"I brought it myself because I wanted to ask you a few questions," explained Knox.

"Yeah?" asked Roger.

Knox nodded. "You said you thought you saw something at the game," he reminded Roger.

"Yeah," replied Roger. "Angels. Real ones."

"Why do you think there would be real angels at the ball game?" asked Knox.

"I dunno," said Roger. "Maybe because I wished for them?"

Knox paused. This is crazy, he thought to himself. He considered turning and walking away, but something in Roger's face made him stay.

This kid was serious.

"What religion are you, kid?" he asked Roger.

"I'm not sure," replied Roger. "Does it matter?"

"Obviously not," Knox said thoughtfully. "So you prayed?"

"To God to help me out," explained Roger. "Nothin' you were doing was helping, so I didn't see how it could hurt."

J.P., who was so shy he kept staring at the sidewalk, giggled. Knox became embarrassed.

"Can the little squirt talk?" Knox asked Roger.

" 'Course he talks," said Roger. "He just doesn't like strangers."

"Me either," said Knox. "I don't even like my friends. These angels you thought you saw. Do you suppose they're coming back?"

"I dunno," said Roger with honesty. "Depends . . ."

"On what?"

"On if they feel like it, I guess."

Knox paused again. "This *is* crazy," he said. Then he looked at Roger's face. The boy was serious.

The Angels were so far behind, Knox decided he didn't have anything to lose by taking a way-out chance like this. "Strike that," he continued. "What I meant to say was, you want to come to the game tomorrow? I have two open seats next to the dugout. Maybe having you there will help us. You could get Aunt Maggie, or whoever she is, to come along."

Roger was very excited but tried his best not to show it. "Maggie doesn't like baseball," he said. "What about J.P.?"

"Okay," agreed Knox. "He can come, too."

7 ▸ A Silly Signal

The Angels' next game was against the Oakland Athletics. As Knox had promised, Roger and J.P. had front-row seats next to the Angels dugout.

During the warm-up Knox emerged from the bullpen and climbed up to where the kids were seated. His assistant, David, was working his way out of the row to the aisle, dragging J.P. along by the hand. A squirt of mustard had somehow landed on the front of his always-clean suit, and he was pretty angry about it.

"What happened to you?" asked Knox.

"It's those kids," he whispered to his boss. Then David explained how J.P. accidentally squirted him with hot dog mustard and that now he was on his way back to the concession stand to buy both kids their second round of junk food. "They're evil," he added.

"Who cares?" said Knox. "The big kid might be lucky. So keep 'em happy."

"Kids don't like me," said David as he climbed the stairs with J.P. "They never like me. Even when I was a kid other kids didn't like me."

When David was gone, Knox stared over at Roger. "Hey, think we'll win today?" he called.

"Maybe," replied Roger.

"Maybe?"

"Hey, I dunno," Roger said with a shrug. "It's your team."

"Don't remind me," moaned Knox. Then he returned to the dugout.

Roger looked out at the field. The Angels were out there, warming up, getting ready for the game. Despite their win they didn't look like much of a team. Roger knew their only hope was the mysterious angels that had helped them last time.

He only wished he could be certain that the angels would come back.

He reached down and brought his soda to his lips. When he lifted the cup he caught sight of something swirling inside it. At first he thought a fly had landed on one of the ice cubes. But when he looked again he recognized the face of Al, the head angel.

Al's face was looking back at him from inside the ice cube!

"No! Please!" begged Al jokingly. "Don't drink me!"

Startled, Roger jumped to his feet and sent his soda cup flying through the air. The soda droplets shot up out of the cup, and as they descended through the air they magically began to blend together until they transformed into the full-size figure of Al himself. Now Al was sitting right next to Roger, in J.P.'s seat.

"Shhh," said Al. "This is between you and me, little guy."

Roger looked at Al dumbfounded. He was speechless.

"No one can see me but you, remember?" continued the head angel. "Sit down already!"

Roger slowly sank back into his seat.

"I left in a hurry the other day," explained Al. "I forgot to tell you a few of the rules. Número uno: don't tell *anyone* about us. Now, I heard you already tell the little kid and el capitán. But *nobody else!* We hate recognition. We're a very sensitive group. If people know we're around, I wouldn't be able to get an angel within a mile of this team!!!"

"Okay," agreed Roger cautiously. "Are you going to help out today?"

"We'll see," replied Al. "We never make commitments. We come and go. Go and come. We're a capricious crowd."

"What's 'capri-sus'?" asked Roger.

Al smiled. "Unpredictable!" he explained. "Just keep your chin up. Your eyes open. And enjoy the game!"

Al thinned into a wisp and vanished. Roger was still staring at the empty seat by the time J.P. returned and sat in it.

"I just saw the big angel," Roger told his friend. "He was sittin' right here. He's gone now."

"Next time will you tell me sooner?" asked J.P. eagerly. "I'd like to try to see one."

Roger waved at the dugout, frantically trying to get Knox's attention. Knox ran up the dugout stairs and to Roger's seat.

"Yeah?" he asked.

"An angel was just here!" said Roger.

"You saw an angel?" asked Knox.

"Yup," replied Roger. "In my soda cup."

Knox crinkled his eyebrows in disbelief.

"In your soda cup?" he repeated skeptically. "Oh-kay . . . Look, ah . . . I've got to get back to the dugout."

"So what do I do if I see another one?" asked Roger.

"Kid," began Knox, "I was thinking of you as a sort of good luck charm. Not as someone who spiritually hallucinates!"

"What's that mean?" asked Roger. He wondered if Knox believed in the angels after all.

"It means if you see anything weird, keep it to yourself!"

"But you should know," insisted Roger. "You're the manager!"

Knox paused. Roger looked hurt. "Okay," he said. "Calm down. In baseball we've got signals. Make some kind of signal. I can't come over here every two seconds."

Roger thought for a moment, then began to flap his arms like a bird. "I'll go like this," he said. "It's an angel sign."

"Okay. Fine," said Knox. "You do that." Then he turned back toward the dugout. At that moment David returned from the concession stand with a tray of gooey cheese nacho chips.

"And we can't let David know," Roger shouted after Knox.

"You're right. Absolutely," Knox muttered back. He had no intention of letting *anybody* know.

Meanwhile, David inched his way down the row. As David neared his seat, J.P. stood up to let him by. But J.P. stood too fast and knocked the food tray out of David's hands. Eagerly J.P. bent down, picked up the tray of nachos, and placed them on the seat next to him. It was David's seat.

51

David hadn't seen where J.P. had placed the nachos. Seconds later, he sat down right on top of all that gooey cheese.

CRUNCH!

Roger and J.P. began to giggle. Soon their giggles broke out into a roaring laugh. David got up. Cheese was hanging from the seat of his pants. Annoyed, he silently walked past the boys and up the stairs that led back to the concession stand.

He had to buy a new tray of nachos.

The game began about half an hour later. The first three innings were dull, uneventful. There were no runs for either side.

It was now the bottom of the fourth, and the Angels were at bat. Knox paced back and forth in the dugout. He was yelling curse words at the team, just as he had been doing since the beginning of the game. He was telling them what a no-good lousy bunch of amateurs they were and how a Little League team could play better than they could.

Knox was yelling pretty loudly, and Roger could hear him.

Roger signaled to Knox. Knox stepped away from the dugout.

"Yeah?" Knox called out.

Roger pointed to David, who wasn't supposed to learn anything about the angels.

"Go buy the kids more nachos," Knox ordered David.

David's face curdled with fear. "Anything but nachos," he begged Knox. "Those little—"

"Then go buy them Angels jackets," said Knox.

"But it's too *hot* out to be wearing jackets," replied David.

"NOW!" ordered Knox. And with that, David disappeared up the stairs and into the crowd.

Roger leaned over the railing. "Four innings," he whispered to Knox. "And no real angels. I've been thinking. Maybe you shouldn't swear so much. I bet the angels don't like it."

Knox stared at Roger for a moment. He couldn't imagine getting through a whole game without uttering one single curse word.

But for the sake of the game he knew he had better try.

Five innings later, in the bottom of the ninth, the score was still 0–0. The Angels were at bat again, but most of the players were slumped on the bench. They looked tired and depressed, as if they didn't care whether they won or lost.

From his seat in the first row, Roger stared

at the dugout. A second before, Danny Hemmerling had been sitting alone on the bench. Now there was someone sitting next to him. And it wasn't another player.

It was an angel, and Roger was the only one who could see him.

8 ◆ An Angel
in the Dugout

"OH, WOW!" shouted Roger as he leaped up from his seat.

"What happened?" asked J.P., so startled he nearly spilled his soda.

"There's someone with Hemmerling," Roger whispered to his friend. He turned to David. He knew he had to get him out of earshot so he could warn Knox. "I need a drink," he told the harried assistant.

"You have a drink," replied David. "Two of them!"

"Not those," insisted Roger. "I need something else. Coffee. I've got to have coffee."

"You drink coffee?" David asked suspiciously.

" 'Course I do," replied Roger. "All the time."

"Yeah, all the time," echoed J.P. "What do you think we are? Little kids or somethin'?"

"Okay, okay," moaned David. "I'll get you coffee. How do you take it?"

"In cups," said Roger confidently.

Grumbling, David rose to his feet and headed off toward the concession stand. As soon as he was gone, Roger turned toward the dugout and began to flap his arms wildly. It was the signal he and Knox had agreed upon should Roger see any angels.

A second later J.P. joined in, also flapping his arms. The two boys looked as if they were about to take off like birds.

Knox looked up from the dugout and saw the signal. He walked over to the railing.

"What's going on?" he asked the boys.

"There's an angel," Roger whispered excitedly. "With Hemmerling!"

"What?"

"There's an *angel* sitting with Hemmerling!" Roger repeated.

Knox glanced into the dugout. He didn't see any angel.

"This is ridiculous," he said to Roger. "I don't know what you're seeing, but there's no one sitting with Hemmerling."

"Yes there *is*!" Roger said insistently.

"And what should I do about it?" asked Knox.

"Put him in!" said Roger. "Pinch-hit!"

"But I got Mitchell coming up," replied Knox. "He's my best hitter! Hemmerling can't

56

hit the broadside of a barn. I can't substitute my worst hitter for my best!"

"If you want a hit, you'll let Hemmerling bat!!!"

"That's crazy!" shouted Knox. "Wacko! You can forget it!"

Knox stormed back to the dugout. He looked at the players slumped there. To his eyes, they were a sorry group. He suddenly wondered how much of a difference it would make if he took a chance and changed the lineup.

Probably none at all, he realized.

"You're up, Hemmerling," he said, pointing to the infielder.

Ray Mitchell jumped up in surprise.

"What're you talking about?" Mitchell asked Knox.

"Yeah," echoed Hemmerling with equal surprise. "What're you talking about?"

"You heard me," said Knox, pointing to both players. "You're out, and you're in."

There was a murmur among the crowd as Danny Hemmerling emerged from the dugout and moved to the batter's box. Hemmerling was known for his speed and glove but definitely not for his bat.

"Hemmerling for Mitchell?" the fans

yelled angrily from their seats. "What are ya? Crazy?"

Roger's eyes narrowed as he watched Hemmerling. He knew that if the fans could see what he saw, they wouldn't be so angry.

An angel was standing right next to him.

Hemmerling positioned himself at home plate. He spread his feet apart and raised his bat. The first pitch came, but he didn't swing.

It was a strike. The crowd began to boo and hiss.

The catcher threw the ball back to the pitcher's mound. Then the pitcher threw a fastball. Again Hemmerling didn't move.

It was another strike.

Knox buried his head in his hands. He wondered if he had done the right thing. At the same time Roger was watching from his seat. He could see that the angel was looking for a way to help Hemmerling get a hit. But if Hemmerling was too nervous to even swing at the ball, how could he do it?

Roger watched as the pitcher wound up for the third pitch and let the ball go hard and fast. Then he saw the angel fly away from Hemmerling and meet the ball in midair as it traveled. The angel reached out and grabbed the ball, slowing it down as it approached home plate.

This time Hemmerling bunted. With the

help of the angel, the ball bounced across the infield. When the pitcher charged for the ball it miraculously leaped over his head.

Stunned, Hemmerling ran to first base while the crowd cheered him on.

The ball continued flying across the field in the direction of third base. But as soon as the third baseman reached up to grab it, it twisted away and headed off in a different direction.

Hemmerling saw his opportunity and charged toward second base.

The ball now seemed to have a life of its own. The pitcher and the other infielders chased after it, but anytime they got close to it, it changed direction.

Seeing that the coast was clear, Hemmerling ran to third base. Then he kept going.

He was trying to make it home.

Just then the angel dropped the ball and let it roll freely across the infield. The shortstop scooped it up and fired it straight toward home plate.

It was a race between Hemmerling and the ball. Hemmerling hurled himself forward. Both he and the ball seemed to reach home plate at the same time.

The crowd was silent as it waited for the umpire's decision. Then the ump spread out his arms and made the call.

Hemmerling was safe at home.

The audience cheered. The Angels had won again, 1–0.

"We won!!!" exclaimed Roger and J.P., jumping up and down.

Roger looked down at the field. Hemmerling's teammates were crowding around him on the field. They slapped him on the back and shook his hand. Hemmerling looked more surprised than any of them.

Roger scanned the field with his eyes in search of the angel, but he was nowhere in sight. Then he looked up at the sky. A single cloud floated over the stadium. It hadn't been there a moment ago.

Roger blinked. When he opened his eyes the cloud was gone, just as mysteriously as it had appeared. He wondered if it wasn't a cloud at all but an angel in disguise.

Roger and J.P. watch the California Angels baseball game for free from their perch in a tree.

Angels manager George Knox's bad temper isn't helped by his team's losing streak.

From the broadcast booth, announcer Ranch Wilder enjoys making his old archrival—George Knox—the laughingstock of the major leagues.

Angels owner Hank Murphy warns Knox about his tantrums on the field.

Roger's father is going off on the open road, dashing Roger's hopes that they can be a family.

Al, an angel only Roger can see, arrives to help the team win some games.

Outfielder Ben Williams makes a spectacular catch!

David Montaine can't help getting J.P.'s food and drink all over his clothes.

Whenever Roger sees a real angel on the field, he signals Knox by flapping his arms.

Ranch Wilder finds out about the angels from J.P. — and soon everyone knows.

Mel Clark takes the mound for the last time in the season finale against the White Sox.

Roger's prayers for a family are answered when Knox decides to adopt him *and* his pal, J.P.

9 ◆ Good-bye, Miguel

After the game, Knox brought Roger and J.P. into his office and closed the door.

"So," Knox said to Roger. "You were right about Hemmerling. He came through."

"Because of the angel," said Roger.

"Whatever," said Knox. He still had the tone of a nonbeliever.

"We've got angels helping the team," Roger insisted.

"Something's happening," agreed Knox. "We know that. We're winning."

It was getting late, and Knox had agreed to get the boys home by five o'clock. But first he brought the boys to a souvenir stand and let them have their pick of Angels caps, pennants, baseballs, and autographed team photos. Soon their little arms were overflowing with mementos from their day at the ball game.

Afterward, Knox led the boys to the staff parking lot. By then he had decided that the

61

boys should watch all the games for the rest of the season.

"When we're on the road you can watch the games on TV," he explained as they weaved their way through the parking lot. "And we'll figure out a way for us to talk on the phone."

"You mean that phone in the dugout that you're always shouting into and banging against the wall and spitting at and stuff?" asked Roger.

"Yeah, yeah, yeah, that phone," Knox answered.

"Cool!" exclaimed Roger.

"Yeah, cool!" echoed J.P.

They arrived at a very expensive-looking sports car. Knox opened the door.

"Get in," he told the boys.

J.P. didn't move.

"C'mon," said Knox. "We don't have all day."

"J.P. won't ride in cars," explained Roger.

"This isn't a car," said Knox. "This is a Porsche."

"He can't do it," said Roger.

J.P. remained frozen.

"What's the problem?" asked Knox. "He gets carsick?"

"Sort of."

"He can puke out the window," said Knox.

He was starting to get impatient. "He won't be the first. Get in!"

Roger stepped closer to Knox. "He used to live in a car with his mom," he explained in a whisper. "He slept in the front seat all curled up like a cat or something. Anyway, now when he gets in a car, his stomach starts to ache."

Knox rolled his eyes. "You can't be serious," he said with a groan.

But try as they might, neither Roger nor Knox could coax J.P. into the car. Finally Knox led the two boys to the players entrance of the stadium. Nearby was an enormous bus with the name California Angels across its side in big bold letters.

J.P. had no trouble getting on the team bus. Both he and Roger climbed aboard with excitement. As Knox drove them through the city streets, their smiling faces beamed proudly at any passersby who might see them through the windows.

A short while later they arrived at Maggie's house. Knox swung the bus door open and let Roger and J.P. off.

"I'll call you tomorrow," he said.

"Okay," said Roger as he and J.P. headed for the house.

J.P. looked back at Knox. "Thank you for the ride home," he said.

Knox raised his brow in surprise. "He speaks," he said to J.P. with a smile.

Then J.P. ran to catch up with Roger.

Maggie was waiting in the living room when the boys burst into the house. She could tell they were bubbling over with excitement at having been to the game.

"You had fun?" she asked.

"A blast!" exclaimed Roger.

"We won!" said J.P. happily.

"Where's Miguel?" asked Roger. He glanced around the living room. "We brought him all kinds of stuff."

"Miguel got placed in a foster home this afternoon," Maggie said gently.

Roger and J.P. looked at each other. They had become good friends with Miguel. Now he was gone, and they would probably never see him again.

"Miguel's gone. . . ," J.P. said sadly. Tears were starting to form in his eyes.

"Where?" Roger asked Maggie. "With whom?"

"A nice family," said Maggie. "They're from Northridge."

"I'm going to miss him!" said J.P. Now he was crying. "I really liked Miguel!"

J.P. ran into the bedroom and shut the door behind him.

Roger looked at Maggie and tried not to show how bad he was feeling. He supposed he always knew that someday he would have to say good-bye to Miguel, and he realized that it also meant that one day he would have to do the same with J.P.

He didn't want to think about it.

"My house is just a place to stay until a permanent family can be found for you boys," Maggie reminded him. "I'm only licensed for short-term care. Miguel had been here for seven months. You understand, don't you, Roger?"

"Yeah," said Roger. He could see that Maggie missed Miguel, too. He placed his arm around her shoulder. "Don't feel bad. I bet we'll see him again."

Later that night Roger and J.P. lay in their beds wide awake. With Miguel gone, the room felt lonelier.

"Roger. . . ," said J.P.

"Yeah."

"Are you asleep?"

"If I was asleep, how would I be talking?"

"You could be sleep-talking," replied J.P.

Roger groaned. "I'll give you a dime tomorrow if you don't say another word," he offered.

"Okay," said J.P. "Roger?"

"You can forget the dime."

"You think your parents are ever going to come get you?"

For a moment Roger remained silent.

"My mom's not alive," he told J.P. "But my dad's going to come back. I'm sure of it."

"You think my mom's ever going to come get me?" asked J.P.

"Maybe," Roger said. "It could happen."

"Yeah. It *could* happen," said J.P. with a smile. "Roger?"

"What?"

"I'm happy you see angels."

"Me, too."

For a long time Roger stared up at the ceiling and thought of the angels. Suddenly he wasn't sad anymore. Instead, he became full of hope. The angels had the power to do miracles. Already they had helped the California Angels win two games. He wondered if, somehow, they had helped Miguel find a family.

Thinking of things in that way made Roger feel better. If miracles were possible, then he knew they could also happen to him.

He was almost certain that his dad would be coming back.

10 ◆ A Surprise Starter

A few days later Roger and J.P. were picked up by David, who was now wearing a see-through plastic rain suit over his regular clothes. This time he was taking no chances that he would suffer another barrage of mustard and nacho stains.

The Angels and the Detroit Tigers were warming up as Roger and J.P. took their seats beside the dugout. As soon as he sat down, Roger noticed something on the field.

"I see an angel," he whispered to J.P.

"Already?" asked J.P. He squinted his eyes at the field in search of the angel. He didn't see a thing. Then he turned to David. He knew he had to get David away from the stands so Roger could signal to Knox.

"I've got to go to the bathroom," J.P. told David. "And I can't go alone. Bad guys might get me."

"Can't you wait a few minutes?" asked David. "We just sat down."

"I've got to go now. Sorry."

David grumpily got up and led J.P. up the stairs. As soon as they were gone, Roger stood up and began to flap his arms. Knox, seeing Roger's signal from the dugout, walked over to the railing.

"What's up?" he asked the boy.

"We got an angel," said Roger with excitement.

"But the game hasn't even started—"

"He's with Mel Clark," Roger said, pointing to the field.

Knox looked over at the bullpen. Mel Clark was sitting on the bench watching the other pitchers warm up.

Knox could see no angel with Clark.

"Impossible," said Knox.

"He's there," insisted Roger. "That means Mel Clark should pitch today."

"Mel's arm's gone," said Knox. "He couldn't throw ten decent pitches to save his life."

"It doesn't matter," said Roger. He watched as a tall, lanky angel stood beside Clark, studying the pitchers' throws. "He should start the game."

"No way," said Knox. "Besides, he's not even on the active roster!"

68

"If the angel pitches with Mel, he'll be awesome," said Roger.

Knox paused and studied Clark. "You really see something?" he asked Roger.

"Yeah. I do."

Knox looked at Roger's face. The boy looked so sincere it was hard not to believe him. Besides, Roger had been right when he made the calls at the Angels' last few games.

Knox walked along the fence to the bullpen and approached Clark. They exchanged some words. Clark's mouth dropped open in surprise. From the stunned look on Clark's face, Roger could tell that Knox had just put him in the game.

As the game began, Clark walked nervously out to the pitcher's mound. He adjusted his glove, his cap, and his belt. Then he let out with one of his long smoker's coughs.

Clark rubbed some sweat away from his chin. He had been begging Knox to put him back in the lineup ever since his arm had healed. Now he was starting the game. He wondered if he still had the right stuff.

Roger and J.P. watched as Clark threw a few warm-up pitches. His throws were hesitant and uneven. Between each throw he had to pause to cough and catch his breath. To the rest of the crowd, Mel Clark did not look like the kind of player whom they could root for.

But Roger knew different. Right behind Clark was an angel.

Clark signaled that he was ready to throw the first pitch, and the first batter for the Tigers came up to the plate. Clark waited, nervously rubbing the baseball with his fingers. Then he brought his arm back and threw the ball.

At that very moment the angel raised his arms and began to flap his wings. Soon the ball was propelled forward on a gust of magical wind.

ZOOM! The ball whizzed by the batter and smacked straight into the catcher's glove.

"Strike!" called the umpire.

The crowd cheered. Roger and J.P. slapped each other with a high five.

Mel Clark smiled to himself. He threw the next pitch. Again the angel flapped his wings. This time the ball curved just as the batter swung. Strike two. The stunned fans cheered. The batter was so surprised that he struck out on the next pitch.

For the rest of the game Mel Clark pitched like a player half his age. His form was elegant and self-assured. He threw fastballs, curve balls, slow balls, and sinkers. He struck out a slew of batters. Those who managed to get on base, he either picked off with precise throws or erased by getting the next batter to hit into a double play.

Before long it was the top of the ninth inning. The Angels were ahead 1–0. The Tigers had two outs and two strikes.

Mel pitched. The ball zoomed toward home plate. Then, just as the batter swung, the ball dipped and landed in the catcher's glove.

That was it. The Angels had won again.

From his seat in the press box, Ranch Wilder watched the frenzy in the stadium in amazement. The fans were cheering wildly. The Angels rushed the pitcher's mound and lifted Mel Clark onto their shoulders. Then they carried him around in a victory parade.

Wilder was suspicious. He wondered how all this was possible. First there was that fantastic catch made by Ben Williams against the Blue Jays. And then, in that same game, Triscuit Messmer hit the ball so hard he broke his bat in two. On top of that, in their game against the Oakland A's, Danny Hemmerling laid down the most amazing bunt in the history of baseball.

And today the game was won by Mel Clark, a pitcher who hadn't started a game in years.

Something strange was going on.

Ranch Wilder decided right then and there that he was going to find out just what it was.

◆ 11 ◆ Softball Kids

After the game, Knox led Roger and J.P. to the team bus. Roger and J.P. had big-time smiles on their faces. And for the first time since they had known him, so did Knox.

"We won!" said J.P.

"Yup," said Roger. "We're on a roll!"

"I feel . . . good," said Knox. He had gotten so used to feeling bad that the words felt strange.

"Me, too," said Roger.

"Me, three," added J.P.

"I owe you guys," said Knox as they reached the team bus. "You name it. Anything you want and you got it."

Roger and J.P. exchanged excited glances. There *was* something Knox could do for them—something they had wanted to ask him since they first met him.

They wanted to play softball.

Knox agreed. Thirty minutes later they

were standing in the center of the vacant lot across the street from Maggie's house. Knox was surrounded by neighborhood kids of all ages, each one taking up a different position on a makeshift softball field. Roger was kneeling behind a dented metal trash can lid, playing catcher. J.P. stood in front of him holding a bat that was nearly as big as he was.

Knox was pitching.

"Elbow up!" Knox shouted to J.P. "Here it comes!"

Knox threw the oversize softball underhanded. J.P. stepped in and swung, hitting the ball. The ball popped straight up, and J. P. ran to first base—a worn rubber tire.

"Great hit, J.P.!" said Knox. "Who's up next?"

A group of kids pushed over each other to get to the bat, but Knox had his eye on one boy in particular who was standing on the hood of a nearby car. The boy was shyly raising his hand.

"Let's give the kid on the car a shot," said Knox. Something about the boy reminded him of himself when he was a child. "What's your name?"

"Marvin Vincent Archer," said the boy as he walked over to home plate.

"You play much ball, Marvin?" asked Knox.

"Never played any ball," replied Marvin. He picked up the bat.

"Okay," Knox said patiently. "Grip the bat with both of your hands. Stand at an angle. Keep your eyes on the ball, and when I say 'Now' I want you to swing."

Marvin nodded and positioned himself just the way Knox had described. Knox took a few steps closer to the boy, then all the outfielders did the same.

Knox tossed the ball.

"Now!" he shouted.

Marvin swung, whacking the softball hard. The ball sailed in the air, flew straight over the fielders' heads, and hit the fence at the far end of the vacant lot.

Marvin ran like crazy to first base. J.P. advanced to second. Knox smiled. He knew there was something about Marvin that reminded him of himself. He jaunted over and gave the boy a high five.

"Great hit, Marvin," said Knox.

A wide smile spread across Marvin's face.

"Okay," said Knox. "Now stay on base and do just what I say."

Marvin nodded eagerly. Knox returned to the pitcher's spot. One of the other kids, the biggest of the bunch, was waiting at home plate, bat in hand.

Knox pitched. The big kid swung and slammed the ball halfway across the lot. J.P. sprinted to third base and then home. Marvin, however, remained frozen at first. He was waiting for Knox's instructions.

"Go, Marvin!" shouted Knox. "Run home!"

Marvin nodded. Then he turned around and ran out of the lot and down the street until he was out of view.

Knox stood watching from the pitcher's spot. He was confused.

"What happened?" he asked aloud.

"You said run home," explained Roger. "He did!"

Knox scratched his head. From all around him came the sound of kids laughing. Then the silliness of the situation sunk in, and he began to laugh, too.

It was the first time he had laughed at anything all season.

Sometimes It Looks Like an Angel, Sometimes It's Not

Week after week the headlines in the newspapers read ANGELS WIN AGAIN! MEL CLARK MAKES COMEBACK! UNSTOPPABLE ANGELS! ANGELS' WINNING STREAK CONTINUES!

On the afternoon the Angels were playing the New York Yankees, the stadium was more crowded than usual. As Roger and J.P. made their way to their specially reserved seats they saw that the stands were filled top to bottom with fans. Some held banners that read We Love You, Angels.

It was clear from the first pitch that the Yankees didn't stand a chance. The Angels executed a fabulous series of double plays, triple plays, fastballs, curve balls, and sinkers. There were slides, home runs, and walks.

The Angels were playing better than ever before.

Only Roger could see how they were doing it. Only his eyes could see the lithe, heavenly angels who lifted and pushed the players, helped stop hits, and assisted with catches and slides. Only Roger was able to signal George Knox to tell him which player had an angel with him and which one didn't.

At one point during the middle of the game, Roger looked over at the scoreboard and saw Al, the head angel, looking down at the field and smiling as his angels helped Knox's Angels score run after run after run.

Even Knox was beginning to show high spirits. With each winning play, he patted his players on their backs or congratulated them by shaking their hands or throwing them a high five. A feeling of goodwill was everywhere.

The California Angels seemed to be unbeatable.

"The Angels have closed out the season with an incredible winning streak," Ranch Wilder said into a microphone as he stood in the center of Anaheim Stadium. "Who would have believed that this team could go from last place at the All-Star break to just one win away from the division title?"

Roger and J.P. were eating breakfast the next morning watching a broadcast of Wilder on television. They had just woken up and were still wearing their matching official Angels pajamas.

"Now it all comes down to the last two games of the season," continued Wilder. "And they are against the defending champion Chicago White Sox, who are one game back and closing fast in a determined effort to deny the Angels the championship! The first of these crucial games takes place right here, this afternoon!"

On the table next to the television set, a fax machine let out with a series of beeps, and a piece of paper began to squeeze its way out through the receiving slot. Roger reached over and grabbed the fax.

"What's it say?" asked J.P. A drop of milk dribbled down the side of his mouth.

"They'll get us at twelve," read Roger. "And he's gonna go with Sanford unless we think they should start someone else."

"Sanford is good," said J.P. thoughtfully. "Don't you think?"

Roger chewed on his cereal. "He's had five days of rest," he said, sounding like a real team manager. "Hasn't had a real angel around in a while, but still, he's tough under pressure. We'll go with Sanford for now."

Just then Maggie walked into the kitchen. She had just gotten off the telephone.

"Roger," she began, "that was your social worker."

Roger stopped chewing. "What did she want?" he asked somberly.

"Your hearing has been changed to this afternoon," Maggie told him.

Roger jumped up from his chair. "But I've got a game this afternoon!" he exclaimed.

"I know," said Maggie. "And I did everything I could to get them to reschedule. But it's not possible."

"I'm not going!"

"You don't have a choice, sweetheart."

"But what about the team?" asked Roger. "What about Knox? What about the pennant?"

"I'll call Mr. Knox and explain," said Maggie. "I know he thinks you boys are his lucky charms, but this is something you have to do. J.P. can go to the game, and we'll try as hard as we can to get you there before it's over."

Roger didn't say anything. He couldn't. He knew that Maggie was right and that there was nothing he could do about it.

◆ 13 ◆ No Miracles Today

That afternoon J.P. sat patiently in his seat in the stands at Anaheim Stadium. Below him he saw the Chicago White Sox take the field and warm up for their game against the Angels.

Beside him was an empty seat—Roger's empty seat.

"When do you think Roger'll be here?" Knox shouted from the field below. J.P. glanced downward. He could tell that Knox was worried.

"Soon," answered J.P. "I hope."

"If we win this game, we win the pennant," said Knox. "I can't believe the kid's not here."

In a short while the game began. In no time at all the White Sox had runners on second and third. Their third-place hitter then drilled a fastball deep into the outfield. Ray Mitchell scrambled for the ball but missed it by a yard. By the time he retrieved it and sent it into the infield, the White Sox had scored two runs.

Knox rubbed the sweat that was beginning to form on his brow. He looked over at the stands and saw that Roger had still not arrived. He climbed the dugout stairs and made his way toward J.P.

David, who was sitting on the other side of J.P., stood up when he saw Knox coming. He knew what he had to do.

"Don't tell me," David said to his boss. "Go get drinks, candy, hot dogs. Just get lost."

Knox nodded, and David made his way down the row and up the stairs.

"Still no Roger," Knox said to J.P.

"He'll be here any second," said J.P. "Maybe."

"Of all the days to haul the kid off to court," groaned Knox. "Why didn't Maggie say he was sick or something?"

"That would be lying," answered J.P. "Maggie would never lie."

"Maggie's not in a pennant race!" Knox snarled. "Hey, you don't see anything, do you, kid?" Knox was hoping for a miracle of any kind.

"Maybe," said J.P. He lifted a pair of binoculars and looked down at the baseball field. For a second he thought he saw some glowing white form. It seemed to be hovering around Ray Mitchell's neck. J.P. smiled excitedly, but before he could say anything Mitchell reached up and pulled a white towel from around his neck.

J.P. frowned. There was no angel after all.

"We've got to face it," said Knox. "You've never seen angels before. Why would you suddenly now?"

"Hey," said J.P. "It *could* happen."

"I don't know who to send in," said Knox in despair. "Or who's going to play well. The most important game of the season and I'm flying blind!"

Knox shook his head and headed back toward the dugout. He was really beginning to worry now.

A few miles away in the downtown family court building, Roger's father sat at a table. At a desk in front of him sat a woman in a dark judicial robe. At the table across from him sat two social workers.

The judge was studying some files in front of her. Then she looked up at Roger's father.

"You understand that once this hearing has established Roger's permanent placement status, his welfare will forever forward be determined by this court."

"I understand," Roger's father said.

"And you have consulted a lawyer?" asked the judge.

"Look, lady," said Roger's father. "I know what I'm doin'. The kid's not going to be mine anymore. I'm not proud of it. But I'm not changin' my mind about it, either."

The judge looked at Roger's father for a long moment. She wanted to give him one last minute to change his mind. When she saw that all he did was hang his head low, she raised up her pen and signed the papers that would separate Roger from his father forever.

Roger's father rose and headed for the courtroom door. When he opened it, Roger and Maggie were waiting in the hallway outside.

"Dad!" exclaimed Roger with surprise. Roger's father kept his eyes low. He was ashamed to look his son in the face.

"I didn't know you were here," continued Roger. "Daddy, the Angels are only one game away from winning the pennant. Can you believe it! Every night I wanted to tell you. It was like you said. They'd—"

But Roger's father turned away from him. "Sorry, boy," he said. Then he hurried down the hall.

"Dad!" Roger called. "Hey, Dad! Did you hear what I said? Dad! Where ya going?"

But by then it was too late. Roger's father

had disappeared out the double doors of the building.

Back at Anaheim Stadium, George Knox marched over to the dugout watercooler and kicked it right off its stand. Then he let out with a string of curse words the likes of which he hadn't used in months. It was the top of the ninth, and his team was being creamed by the White Sox 4–0.

With Roger gone, there seemed no hope for a win.

As the Angels got ready to take the field, Knox had a sudden, desperate thought.

"I'll find the angels myself!" he said aloud. Then he moved to the player closest to him and began feeling the air around him. The rest of the players stopped and looked at him.

Knox looked as if he were losing his mind.

"None of you go anywhere," said Knox. He made his way to each player and waved his hands all around them. "I want all of you to stand up! Now move your arms around your bodies like this!"

The players just stared at him.

"DO IT!" he ordered. "ALL OF YOU! DO IT NOW!"

The players slowly began to do as they were told. Soon the entire stadium could see the players waving their arms about wildly in the dugout. They began to laugh.

"I need to know," Knox told his men. "Does anyone feel anything?"

"Yeah," said Hemmerling. "I feel stupid."

"Does that count?" asked Bass.

"Not for you," quipped another player.

"We got an inning left," said Knox. "Pay attention. There may be some . . . some . . . force out there. It's a force that can help us."

"A force?" asked Williams.

"I missed something," said Bass. "Are we talkin' about a force play?"

"In order to win I have to know *who* has the *force!*" exclaimed Knox.

Eventually the umpire walked over to the dugout and angrily ordered the Angels out onto the field. Knox followed Williams toward the outfield.

"Ben, you gotta let me know if you feel something," he pleaded. "The force has been with you before."

"I'll try," said Williams, perplexed.

Try as they might, the Angels were not able to prevent the White Sox from scoring another run before they got their turn at bat. Once at the plate, all three batters quickly struck out.

A moan of disappointment sounded from

the Angels fans in the stands. The miracle run appeared to be over.

But even though the Angels' winning streak had ended, everyone knew that with one game left to be played in the series against the White Sox, the Angels still had one last chance to win the pennant.

◆ 14 ◆ The Truth

After the game Hank Murphy called Knox into his office. Something had gone wrong, terribly wrong, and he wanted to know what it was.

"What exactly were you doing?" Murphy asked, tilting his huge cowboy hat back off his forehead.

"I was trying to win," Knox explained in a feeble, somewhat embarrassed tone.

"By dancing in the dugout?" asked Murphy.

"I wasn't dancing in the dugout," said Knox, although he didn't know exactly how to explain what he had been doing.

Just then the door opened, and J.P. stuck his head into the room. He had been waiting outside the office for Knox to take him home.

"I'm right in the middle of something, kid!" snapped Knox.

"I . . . feel . . . so . . . bad. . . ," said J.P.

Knox excused himself and went into the

room outside Murphy's office. J.P. had started to cry.

"Ah, c'mon, kid," said Knox. "Don't cry. The last thing I need right now is some kid crying."

"We lost," sobbed J.P.

"Hey, c'mon," Knox said gently. "It's only a game. You're getting snot all over. Stop it."

Knox dropped down on one knee. He wasn't sure how to do it, but he tried comforting J.P. by patting him on the shoulder the way he would a sad puppy.

"It's not your fault," Knox told the boy. "It's nobody's fault."

"I tried to see angels," said J.P. "I really did."

"Look," said Knox. "The angels come for Roger. And without him, well, who knows if they're even out there. I guess without the angels helping, this team doesn't have what it takes. Or maybe . . . I don't have what it takes."

"The team could win without angels," said J.P. "It could happen."

"Maybe," Knox said sadly. "Give me a minute, kid, and I'll be out to take you home."

Knox turned and went back into the office. J.P. sat down on the couch, wiped his nose on his sleeve, and waited. Suddenly he heard somebody else come into the room. He looked up and saw a man standing in front of him with a big friendly grin on his face.

"Hey, I'm Ranch Wilder," said the man. "Voice of the Angels."

Wilder had been walking down the stadium hallway when he heard Knox and J.P. talking in the waiting room. He had heard J.P. say something about seeing angels and wanted to learn more.

"I know who you are," said J.P. It was the first time he had ever seen Wilder in person. "I heard you on the radio. You've got a big chin."

"Everybody's a critic," Wilder said. "Too bad about the loss. Knox took it hard. He was acting pretty crazy out there today."

" 'Cause Roger couldn't come," explained a disappointed J.P.

"If Roger was here," Wilder probed, "you think they would have won?"

"Yeah."

"He's lucky? Is that it?"

"He sees the angels." J.P. had forgotten the rule about not telling anyone about the angels.

Wilder wrinkled his brow. "You think there are real angels out there?"

"Yeah," said J.P. "But I don't see 'em."

"And Knox? He sees them?"

"No," replied J.P. "Roger has to tell him when they're here."

"Really?" asked Wilder with astonishment. "You know, if you truly wanted to help Mr. Knox, you'd tell me all about this angel thing."

J.P. thought for a moment. He felt so bad that the Angels had lost and that Mr. Knox was being yelled at by his boss, Hank Murphy. He wanted to do something to make everything all right. He knew that that's what Roger would want him to do.

So he told Ranch Wilder everything. He told him how Ben Williams made that first outfield catch and how Triscuit Messmer broke his bat in two. He also told him how Roger came up with the signal to let Mr. Knox know when an angel was about to help a player such as Danny Hemmerling or Whit Bass and how Roger told Mr. Knox that Mel Clark should start even when everyone knew Clark's arm was out of shape and he hadn't started in such a long time.

Wilder took out a small notepad and scribbled down everything J.P. said. It was the most fantastic story he had ever heard in his life. In fact, it was the sports scoop of the century.

By tomorrow morning it would be printed in all the newspapers.

15 ◆ I Don't Believe in Angels

Later that evening Knox and J.P. sat in the Angels' bus. It was parked at the curb outside Maggie's house, waiting for Maggie and Roger to get home from family court.

Knox was growing impatient. He had promised Hank Murphy that they would meet and talk about the strategy for the next game.

"I've got to go in five minutes," Knox told J.P. anxiously.

"He's coming real soon," said J.P. "I can feel it."

Just then Maggie's car came down the street and pulled into the driveway. Knox and J.P. climbed out of the bus.

"Took a little longer than you expected," Knox commented as Maggie got out of her car.

"We waited three hours for his hearing," explained Maggie. "That's quick for family court."

"What'd they decide?" asked Knox.

"It was a formality," replied Maggie. "His father officially signed off in July. Roger now belongs to the state of California."

Knox saw J.P. get into Maggie's car and slide next to Roger, who was still sitting in the front seat.

"I thought the kid didn't like cars," Knox said, remembering what Roger had told him.

"The kid likes Roger," said Maggie. Then she started up the steps and went into the house.

Knox looked at J.P. and Roger sitting in the front seat of the car. They looked so helpless and so alone. It made Knox angry that Roger's father had given the boy up. Roger was a good kid. He deserved better.

Knox opened the car door and slid behind the steering wheel. The boys barely looked up at him.

"Roger," Knox began, "I'm sorry about today."

"Why?" Roger asked coldly. His voice was full of hurt. "Because you lost your ball game?"

"No," replied Knox. "Because you're hurt."

"You don't know anything about it!" Roger snapped back.

"I've got an idea what you're going through," said Knox.

"Yeah?!" Roger barked. "Well, an ice-cream cone and a baseball cap aren't going to make me feel better, so why don't you just get out of here!"

"Roger, that's not nice," said J.P. "He didn't mean that, Mr. Knox."

"Yes he did," Knox said knowingly. He was saying it to Roger. "Right now you'd like everyone to just go away."

"You've got that right," said Roger.

"Okay," said Knox. "But that won't make you any less angry."

Roger didn't say anything.

"You know, Roger," Knox continued, "I never saw my dad when I was growing up. He was a drinker. He couldn't take care of himself, so taking care of us was out of the question. Now I'm not sure the pain that that caused ever goes away, but I am sure you shouldn't go through life thinking everyone you ever meet will one day let you down because if you do, a very bad thing will happen. You'll end up like me."

Knox got out of the car and said, "I'm not sitting here all night. I'm hungry. I'm going inside."

J.P. looked up at Knox. "I thought you said you had to be somewhere," he said.

"I do," said Knox. "I've got to be with you guys."

Then Knox climbed the stairs to Maggie's house and went inside.

George Knox cooked dinner for Maggie and the boys that night. After the events of the day, Maggie was grateful to be free of that chore. Afterward, Knox joined J.P. and Roger on the front porch.

Roger was just as quiet and distant as he had been all through dinner.

"Next time I'll try lasagna," said Knox. "You guys like lasagna?"

"No," Roger replied flatly.

"What's lasagna?" asked J.P. "I forget."

"Maggie liked my dinner," said Knox.

"Maggie fell asleep before you even set the table," Roger reminded him.

"But she was real happy," smiled J.P. "Probably 'cause she didn't have to cook."

J.P. glanced up. There was just a sliver of the moon in the night sky.

"Look, up in the sky," J.P. pointed. "God's thumbnail."

"It's only the moon, J.P., " said Roger without even looking up. "There's no God up there."

Knox was astounded. "I can't believe you

said that," he said to Roger. "The kid who sees angels."

Roger looked up at the sky. Suddenly all the events of the day came back to him. He was flooded with feelings of loneliness and hurt. The image of his father walking down the family court hallway and away from him played over and over again in his mind.

What had gone wrong? he wondered. His father wasn't supposed to go away. He was supposed to come back when the Angels won the pennant. And he was *supposed to come back for good.*

"I don't believe in angels," Roger finally said.

"Roger!" exclaimed J.P. with alarm. "What are you talkin' about?"

"It's okay, J.P.," said Knox. "Roger has had a tough day."

And with that, Knox placed his arm around Roger's shoulder. Roger looked up. The look in Knox's eyes surprised him. It was filled with understanding.

16 ◆ Knox on the Spot

Hank Murphy sat behind the desk in his home office. The desk was made out of a giant wagon wheel and fit in perfectly with the Western decor of Murphy's house.

Spread out on the desk in front of him was the morning newspaper. It was open to the sports section. Across the top, the headline read ANGELS MANAGER GEORGE KNOX SEEING REAL ANGELS? Below it, the subheading continued: "Child tells of real angels in the ballpark."

The office door opened, and a polite middle-aged housekeeper ushered George Knox into the room. Knox stood and waited for Murphy to look up at him from the desk.

"You stood me up last night," said Murphy.

"I'm sorry," said Knox. "I meant to come over, but—"

"Forget that," said Murphy. "What in the Sam Hill is all this *real angel* stuff?"

96

"It's nothing," said Knox. He had read the same article earlier that morning.

Murphy tossed the newspaper at Knox angrily.

"You're going over like a stink bomb in the bleachers, pal," he shouted. "Start talking!"

Knox thought for a moment. What could he say? Then he decided. He'd tell the truth. He could think of no other explanation.

"Okay," he started. "There're these two kids. I think of them as mascots. Well, there's just something going on between me and them."

"Anything that happens anywhere near my ball club is my business," snarled Murphy. "Understand?"

"Yes."

Murphy paused and tried to calm himself down.

"So you think these kids see angels?" he asked.

"Just the one kid," replied Knox.

"You're telling me you believe there are real angels in the ballpark?"

"Sometimes," admitted Knox. "But not on all the plays."

Murphy's face was beginning to turn red. "You've lost it, partner!" he said.

"Look," began Knox, "if I lied to you, the

angels wouldn't like it and they might not come back. They're very temperamental."

"The pressure is too much for you," Murphy sighed.

"I know it sounds crazy, but—"

"You're darn right it sounds crazy," Murphy cut in. "You've got a history, and I can't ignore it! I won't have a repeat of Cincinnati!"

"I'm not the same person I was in Cincinnati!" Knox snapped back.

"I wish I could believe that," said Murphy. "Sorry, George, but I'm relieving you of management responsibilities."

"You can't do that!"

"Of course I can," said Murphy. "It's my team."

"But nothing's wrong with me," insisted Knox.

"Prove it!"

"How?"

"Publicly renounce this hogwash," said Murphy. "I'll give you twenty-four hours to get your head back on straight. Then I'll call a press conference. You repeat any of the baloney I heard in here and I'll have someone else running my team. We'd be talking the end of your baseball career. Have I made myself clear?"

Knox was stunned. He had to choose between the truth and his future. For him the choice was clear.

"Yes," he replied in a weak voice. Then he turned and left the office.

Yes, Knox thought to himself as he walked to his car, I'll renounce everything.

Yes, he thought as he drove home, I'll make a public statement denying that real angels helped my team.

17 ◆ The Most Important Belief

That same morning Roger and J.P. sat at the kitchen table too upset to eat their cereal. Roger had already read the morning sports page. Now he was reading it aloud to J.P.

" 'The source said that the boy, known as Roger,' " he read slowly, " 'even watches the games on TV when the team is out of town and reports to manager Knox over the telephone.' "

"What's a 'source'?" asked J.P.

"The person who told," explained Roger. Then he continued to read: " 'And when Mel Clark made his amazing comeback after the All-Star break, it was Roger's idea to start him.' "

"Who do you think told?" said J.P., feeling guilty.

"I dunno," replied Roger.

"This is bad, right?"

"Very bad."

"Are we in trouble?"

"He's in trouble, that's for sure," said Roger

as he pointed to a picture of Knox next to the article.

"My stomach's starting to hurt," complained J.P.

"We've got to do something to help," said Roger. "We're going to have to tell Maggie."

Later that afternoon Roger and J.P. told Maggie the whole story. Once she heard the fantastic tale, the events of the past few weeks began to make sense. Now she knew why George Knox had taken such an interest in Roger and J.P. and why it was so important that they attend each game.

She also began to understand why Roger believed in the angels himself. It seemed as if so much was at stake for him. She realized that by losing his father in family court the day before, he must have lost his belief in miracles, too.

The phone rang just as Roger had finished telling his story. Maggie answered it. It was George Knox.

"He said he doesn't want you at the press conference," she told Roger as she hung up the phone. "He doesn't want to subject you to the publicity, and I think he's right."

"I'm goin'," said Roger with determination.

"Me, too," echoed J.P. just as intently.

101

"No, you're not," Maggie said.

"Maggie, there really were angels," Roger insisted. "I saw them. Don't you believe me?"

Maggie knew that Roger believed in what had happened. Maybe they weren't real angels he saw, but whatever it was, he had believed in them. Still, she didn't want to see him go through another major disappointment.

"I'm not sure what you saw," she replied.

"You told me you believed in miracles!" Roger reminded her.

"I do," said Maggie hesitantly.

"Well, they're going to ask him about the angels," said Roger. "What's he going to say? We've got to help him, Maggie!"

Maggie wasn't sure what to do. The only thing she was certain of was that Roger wanted to help George Knox. He felt responsible for the trouble Knox had gotten into, and he wanted to do something to help him. That made Maggie feel proud.

Maggie got up and took her car keys out of her handbag. Roger and J.P. smiled.

Whether he wanted them to or not, they were going to get George Knox out of his jam.

The conference room at Anaheim Stadium was filled with reporters, television cameras, and bright lights. The entire Angels team was there as well. Everyone was waiting for George Knox to appear and begin the press conference.

Ranch Wilder smiled as he entered the room with his camera crew. He was enjoying his role in making George Knox the laughing-stock of the major leagues.

Suddenly the crowd of reporters turned toward the podium. The back door opened, and Hank Murphy led George Knox up to the microphones.

A hush fell over the room.

"We're going to make this short and sweet," Murphy told the crowd. "My manager, George Knox, has something he'd like to say."

Knox stepped closer to the microphones. He kept his head down and his eyes low. He was embarrassed.

"I have a statement I'd like to make," he said shyly.

He looked up and saw the door open at the far end of the room. Maggie walked in, followed by Roger and J.P. Knox quickly looked away from them.

"I'm going to read my statement," he continued. "And then I'll answer a few questions."

Knox pulled a piece of paper out of his pocket and unfolded it. "There have been re-ports that I have been using angels to help the team win," he began. Then he stopped, unable to continue. He looked at the crowd, but all he could see were the sweet faces of Roger and J.P. looking back at him.

He turned the paper facedown.

"I was going to read a statement," he told everybody. "But instead I'll just shoot from the hip." He glanced behind him. Hank Murphy was throwing him a confused look.

"You know," he said, "there are lots of times in sports when there's no logical explanation for why things happen. Sometimes a player gets hot and goes beyond his or her natural ability. Is that just adrenaline? I don't know. But I have to believe there are times in life where something higher, stronger, maybe even spiritual, is with us."

Knox looked across the crowd at Roger. A smile had spread across the boy's face.

"Last year I lost control of myself and kept my team from realizing its goal in Cincinnati," Knox continued. "But that's not what's going on here. Now, I can't explain it, but something has happened to my players this season. Something has changed the way they play and the way I manage. Call it angels. Call it faith. Call it whatever you want. That's all I have to say."

There was a murmur of confusion from the crowd of reporters. What Knox said was not what they had expected to hear.

"Does that mean you really think a kid sees angels at your games?" Ranch Wilder shouted out.

Knox knew that Wilder was deliberately trying to put him on the spot, trying to make him look foolish. But before he could open his mouth and answer, Maggie pushed her way through the crowd.

"I'd like to say something on George Knox's behalf," she said.

"And who are you?" Hank Murphy asked from the podium.

"My name is Maggie Nelson," Maggie answered. "I take care of foster children. And the two kids I look after are the ones involved in this angel business."

The crowd began murmuring again. Then a series of flashbulbs went off as reporters took Maggie's picture.

"Now, these children could tell you what happened," said Maggie. She was looking down at Roger and J.P. Both boys were smiling back at her, proud as they could be. "But you'd probably just laugh at them. And yet when a pitcher crosses himself before he goes to the mound, no one jokes about that. And when a football player drops to one knee and thanks God after scoring a touchdown, no one laughs about that. Why is it all right to believe in

God but not in angels? Aren't they all on the same team?"

Hank Murphy moved closer to Maggie. "Is it your belief that angels play baseball?" he asked.

"Since the All-Star break?" smiled Maggie. "Yes."

Everyone in the room laughed at that.

"All the children I ever cared for have needed someone to watch over them," explained Maggie. "They've all needed some kind of angel. So I tell them to have faith. To believe. And to look inside themselves. The footprints of an angel are love. Where there is love and belief, miraculous things can happen. That I can prove."

Everyone was silent as Maggie talked. There was something about what she was saying that each person in the room believed.

"I guess what I'm really saying to you," Maggie continued, "is that I believe God works in mysterious ways."

"Well," Hank Murphy began in a humble voice, "at least we agree on that."

"I also want to say something," shouted a voice from the back of the room. Everyone turned to see Mel Clark rise up from his seat.

"I don't know if there are angels out there other than the twenty-five of us in uniform,"

Clark continued, "but I know there's one thing I won't do. I won't play baseball for anyone but George Knox. I believe in him."

"That goes for me, too," said Triscuit Messmer, who stood up and joined Clark.

Soon all the players stood and nodded their heads in agreement with Messmer and Clark.

Knox was overwhelmed. At the beginning of the season he was embittered. Nobody liked him. Now they wouldn't go onto the field without him.

"Thank you," Knox said softly.

Hank Murphy had heard enough. It was one thing to be made a laughingstock in the eyes of the public. He could fix that with a news conference. But it was quite another thing if your team wouldn't play ball for you. No, he thought. That wouldn't do at all.

"That's all, folks," Murphy told the reporters. "Print whatever you want. George Knox is managing this ball club. And if there are angels in the outfield, I just hope they're on our side."

Roger and J.P. jumped out of their seats and cheered. Then they both wrapped their arms around Maggie. Even the reporters seemed to explode with enthusiasm.

Roger's eyes searched the room. Knox was being swept out of the room, engulfed by a sea of people. But Knox's eyes were also searching the room, and soon they locked into Roger's.

Roger smiled at Knox. Sure, the Angels would get to finish out the season. They might even win the pennant, but all that didn't seem as important to Roger as it once did.

What was important was that people *believed*. Okay, maybe they still didn't believe in real angels or miracles. But that was okay just as long as they believed in George Knox.

For Roger, that was the most important belief of all.

18 ◆ Al Says Good-bye

That evening Anaheim Stadium glistened like a jewel under its bright stadium lights. The fans poured in and filled every seat in the stands to watch the deciding game for the pennant. Many were wearing homemade angel wings. Others were sporting hats that had halos stapled to them.

Angel fever was everywhere.

Roger and J.P. arrived dressed in the official Angels ballboy uniforms that Knox had given them. Instead of going to their usual seats beside the dugout, they walked into the dugout itself. Knox had arranged for them to sit with the team during this, the final game.

The Angels were milling about the dugout waiting for the game to begin. Across the field in the other dugout the Chicago White Sox were doing the same. After a few minutes of letting the team warm up, Knox called his players together.

"No matter what happens tonight," he told the team, "all of you are winners. You've proven that to me. So let's go out there and do the best we can. That's what it's really all about. Go get 'em, guys!!!"

The players cheered as the starting lineup charged the field. Several minutes later the national anthem was sung. A second after that, the White Sox sent out their first batter.

Roger scanned the field and the dugout for angels. He had not seen any since he arrived. He did not even see any signs of Al.

By the end of the fourth inning the White Sox held a one-run lead, 3–2.

Knox pulled Roger aside. "Anybody got any . . . you know?" he asked with a wink.

"No," said Roger.

THWACK! A White Sox player smacked a fastball. Knox looked up and saw the Angels bring the inning to an end with a double play.

"That's okay," he said, smiling. "We're holding our own. We're hanging in there."

A few minutes later Knox gathered the team to discuss strategy for the next inning. J.P. got up and walked over to the water fountain for a drink.

Roger was sitting by himself.

"Hey, kiddo," came a familiar voice. "Sharp outfit! Wish I had one!"

Roger looked next to him. Al had finally appeared.

"I'm so glad you're here," Roger said excitedly. "I was worried you guys wouldn't come because a lot of people now know about the angels."

"No one's coming," said Al. "Championships have to be won on their own. It's a rule."

Roger looked confused. "What do you mean?" he asked.

"I came here to check on Mel," he explained. "He's going to be one of us soon."

Roger was shocked. He looked over at Mel Clark, who was huddled with the rest of the team, listening to Knox.

"You mean he's going to—?" began Roger. He could hardly bring himself to say the words.

"He's smoked for years," explained Al. "That's always a mistake. He's got six months left to live, but he doesn't know anything's wrong yet."

"No!" exclaimed Roger. He wanted to cry.

"Don't you worry," said Al. "He's well taken care of. You concentrate on your own life now. We expect great things from you, kid. We'll all be watching. Remember that even though you can't see us. We'll be watching."

And with that, Al got up, turned to the wall, and disappeared right through it.

Roger looked out at the field. Mel Clark had just taken his position on the pitcher's mound to open the next inning. Clark brought his ungloved hand to his lips and tried to hide a short cough.

When Roger saw this his eyes filled with tears.

19 ◆ Knox Knocks the Socks off the Sox

By the bottom of the eighth inning, the game was tied 3–3. The Angels had two outs. If they didn't score at least one run and hold the lead, they could be finished.

Roger watched nervously from the dugout as the game progressed. He knew that there would be no real angels to help the team along this time. If the Angels were going to win, it would have to be on their ability as a ball club and on the managing of George Knox.

Ray Mitchell got up to bat. Roger looked over at Knox, who was sitting at the end of the bench looking at Roger with a pleading expression on his face. He wanted to know if an angel was with Mitchell.

Roger helplessly shook his head no.

Knox quickly rose to his feet.

"You got this one, Ray!" he shouted at home plate. He sounded charged with enthusiasm. "You hear me? You can do it!"

113

Ray looked over at Knox and threw him a thumbs-up. But Roger could see a look of uncertainty in the batter's eyes.

Then the pitch came, and Mitchell swung hard. The ball exploded off his bat with a loud *THWACK!* It sailed higher and higher into the air, way over the fielders' heads and way over the back wall.

The fans went wild in the stands as Mitchell jogged around the bases. The Angels were now ahead by one.

Next, Triscuit Messmer got up to bat. The pitch came, and Messmer missed. Strike one. Then the second pitch came, and Messmer hit a pop fly toward the shortstop.

Messmer headed to first base with all the speed he could muster, but it was to no avail. It was an easy play for the shortstop.

The inning was over.

The Angels took the field as the ninth inning began. Mel Clark stretched his arm. He was still in the game and beginning to look tired.

"You think you can finish this thing?" Knox asked Clark.

Mel let out a small cough and then nodded. Then he ran out to the pitcher's mound.

Roger watched as Clark positioned himself on the mound.

"He's all alone," Roger mumbled sadly.

"Don't worry, Roger," said J.P. with his usual optimism. "An angel will come. Mel always gets an angel."

But Roger knew there would be no more angels for Mel Clark.

Seconds later the first White Sox hitter of the inning got up to the plate. Clark pitched. The batter hit the ball just over the second base bag and ran safely to first.

The second hitter bunted the next pitch back to Clark. Clark scooped up the ball and threw it to first. The hitter was out, but the man on first had now advanced to second base. The sacrifice had worked.

Clark turned back toward the batter's box to face the next batter. He wound up and threw a sinker. The batter swung and hit a grounder between second and third base. The White Sox runner remained at second while Garcia, the shortstop, picked up the ball and fired it to first.

But the throw was late. The White Sox now had men on first and second.

Mel Clark was dripping with sweat.

In the dugout Knox glanced over at Roger. Roger shrugged. Still no angels.

The next batter positioned himself at the plate. Clark threw it wide. The batter didn't move. The umpire called a ball.

The catcher returned the ball to Clark. Clark studied the batter. Then he wound up and pitched again. This time he threw a fastball. And this time the batter hit it hard. The ball soared into the outfield. It looked like a home run.

The ball approached right fielder Ben Williams. He leaped high into the air, his arm outstretched. The ball touched the tip of his glove and then sank into his palm.

The Angels fans cheered from the bleachers. The White Sox now had two outs. But the runners had advanced to second and third.

Knox nervously wrung his hands together as he watched the next White Sox hitter get up at bat. It was the league RBI leader. Knox then looked over at Clark, who had just turned away from the mound to let out a series of violent, hacking coughs.

Knox turned toward Roger. Roger shook his head again. There were still no angels on the field.

"There's an angel there now, right?" J.P. asked Roger. "One's coming, right, Roger? Right?"

"I dunno," replied Roger. "I don't think so."

A hush fell over the stadium as Clark turned to face the next batter. The Angels were ahead by only one, with two outs at the top of the ninth. Everyone knew the importance of this next at bat, especially Mel Clark.

Clark wound up and released his first pitch. The hitter swung and smashed the ball down the line into the corner—just foul.

The hitter repositioned himself and took a few practice swings. Clark squinted at the catcher's signals as he decided on his next pitch. Then he threw it. Way outside. Ball one.

Then Clark threw another quick pitch. It was also outside. Ball two. This was followed by ball three.

Clark paused and took some deep, heaving breaths. He looked very tired out there.

After a few seconds he wound up and pitched again. This time the batter swung and hit the ball solidly. It was deep but veered off into foul territory again.

Knox stormed over to Roger. "Is anybody with him?" he asked the boy anxiously.

"No," Roger replied. "But maybe you could leave him in anyway?" He knew what Knox must be thinking. With this much at stake, why not pull Clark and replace him with another pitcher?

Knox walked over to Roger and whispered a plan into the boy's ear. Roger smiled in agreement. Knox called for time and strode over to the pitcher's mound. The stands were quiet with anticipation.

"Mel. . . ," Knox said to the pitcher.

Clark sighed. "I got nothing left," he admitted. He was ready to be taken out.

Knox smiled. "Yeah, you do," he told Clark warmly. "You got one strike left."

Clark looked dumbfounded at Knox. Knox looked back toward the dugout and nodded to Roger. Roger stood up and began to flap his arms up and down. It was the signal that a real angel was on the field.

"You got an angel with you right now," Knox told Clark. "He just got here. And he's going to help you."

Clark looked over at the dugout. J.P. had joined Roger and was also flapping his arms.

"The kid sees one?" Clark asked Knox.

"Yeah," said Knox. "He must. That's the signal."

Suddenly all the Angels fans, upon seeing Roger and J.P. in the dugout, rose from their seats and began to flap their arms. For a moment it looked as if they would all begin flying.

"They must feel it, too," Knox told Clark as they both stared awestruck at the fans.

"Okay," Clark said confidently.

"Give 'em your best, Mel," said Knox. "For

the championship. You can do it." Then Knox returned to the dugout.

The crowd cheered when they realized that Clark was staying on the mound.

Roger and J.P. watched as Clark stepped back into position. They became wide-eyed when he wound up and released the ball.

The ball flew toward the batter's box as fast and as straight as any Roger and J.P. had ever seen Mel Clark throw. Without any movement on the ball, the White Sox batter had no trouble pounding it head-on.

ZOOM! The ball rocketed right toward the pitcher's mound. Clark dived with his glove arm extended. The ball landed at the tip of his glove just as he hit the ground in a cloud of dirt. There was so much dust that it was hard to see if Clark had caught the ball.

Then the dust cleared. Clark was still on the ground with his arm extended. Cradled snugly in the pocket of his glove was the ball.

The White Sox were out. The Angels had won!

Roger and J.P. leaped into the air and cheered along with a stadium full of fans.

"The Angels won the pennant," Roger said shocked. He just couldn't believe it.

The Angels rushed onto the field as Clark rose to his feet. There were tears in his eyes as his teammates lifted him up, hoisted him on their shoulders, and marched him around the field for everyone to see before carrying him back to the dugout.

"We did it!" Clark shouted to Knox. "The angel was there with me."

"No, Mel," explained Knox with a smile. "We just wanted you to believe. No one was there. You did it by yourself!"

Clark dropped his jaw in astonishment as he realized that he had won the game with no help at all. He had won it solely on his own skill.

◆ 20　A Family Again

"We won! Maggie, we won!!!" shouted J.P. as he burst through the front door of Maggie's house. Maggie was waiting for the boys in the living room with her arms outstretched.

"I heard," replied Maggie as Roger and J.P. rushed to give her a hug. "Congratulations!"

"The Angels won the pennant," said Roger. But his voice was wistful and sad. Winning the pennant hadn't been enough.

Just then Knox entered the house. He and Maggie looked at each other as if they had a secret.

"Social Services called today, Roger," said Maggie.

"What'd they want?" asked J.P. He was fearful of Roger being moved away.

Roger's face brightened. "Was it about my father?" he asked.

"No," replied Maggie. "But it was about being placed in a permanent home."

121

At those words a tear streamed from J.P.'s eye. Then he took off down the hall and ran into his bedroom. Maggie chased after him.

Roger just stood in the center of the living room. He remained quiet and thoughtful. It looked like he would be getting a family after all, but not the one he wanted. It wouldn't be with his own father.

Just then Knox took Roger by the shoulders and turned him around. He knelt down and looked the boy straight in the eye.

"Nothing is probably ever as good as your real parents," Knox began gently. "But other people could love you, too, and take care of you."

"Yeah," said Roger without much conviction. "I guess. . . ."

"Roger," continued Knox, "the person who called Social Services—that was me. I want you to come live at my house. I want to try to be a dad."

Roger looked at Knox with disbelief. He realized that this was what he had wanted all along. He felt Knox would make the best dad a kid could ever have.

But something held him back from showing his excitement.

"I . . . I . . . can't," replied Roger sadly. "I

122

mean, thank you and everything, but I gotta stay here."

Knox was stunned. "Why?" he asked.

"I couldn't leave J.P.," replied Roger as he stared down the hallway to the bedroom.

Knox smiled. "I'd never leave J.P.," he said. "I'm petitioning for him, too."

Just then J.P. stuck his head out from the bedroom door.

"I heard that," he said with a smile. Then he and Maggie walked back into the living room to join Knox and Roger.

"But what about Maggie?" asked J.P. "She needs us, too."

"Sweetheart," said Maggie. "Knowing you two have got a good home is what I need."

"Hey," exclaimed Roger with a smile. "We're going to be a family!"

Outside, up in the sky the moon brightened and the stars began to twinkle.